# MUSTACHES
## FOR
# Maddie

# OTHER BOOKS

### BY CHAD MORRIS

*Cragbridge Hall, book 1:*
*The Inventor's Secret*

*Cragbridge Hall, book 2:*
*The Avatar Battle*

*Cragbridge Hall, book 3:*
*The Impossible Race*

### BY SHELLY BROWN
*Ghostsitter*

# MUSTACHES FOR Maddie

## CHAD MORRIS and SHELLY BROWN

SHADOW
MOUNTAIN

Interior mustache images: bekulnis/shutterstock.com.
Photo on page 242 by Kristi Price.

Visit us at ShadowMountain.com

First printing in hardbound 2017
First printing in paperbound 2018

This is a work of fiction. Characters and events in this book are products of the authors' imagination or are represented fictitiously.

**Library of Congress Cataloging-in-Publication Data**
Names: Morris, Chad, author. | Brown, Shelly, author.
Title: Mustaches for Maddie / Chad Morris and Shelly Brown.
Description: Salt Lake City, Utah : Shadow Mountain, [2017] | Summary: "Inspired by a true story. Maddie is a normal twelve-year-old, but when an MRI scan reveals she has a brain tumor, it will take all her imagination, courage, and support from her friends and family to meet this new challenge"—Provided by publisher.
Identifiers: LCCN 2016050124 | ISBN 9781629723303 (hardbound) | ISBN 9781629724195 (paperbound)
Subjects: | CYAC: Brain—Tumors—Fiction. | BISAC: JUVENILE FICTION / Social Issues / Emotions & Feelings. | JUVENILE FICTION / Health & Daily Living / Diseases, Illnesses & Injuries. | JUVENILE FICTION / Social Issues / Friendship. | JUVENILE FICTION / Social Issues / Death & Dying.
Classification: LCC PZ7.M827248 Mu 2017 | DDC [Fic]—dc23
LC record available at https://lccn.loc.gov/2016050124

Printed in the United States of America
Lake Book Manufacturing, Inc., Melrose Park, IL

10  9  8  7  6  5  4  3  2  1

*To Maddie Marnae
and all those who prayed
and wore mustaches for her.*

*And to the humble potato she loves.*

# CHAPTER 1

# A Pink Mustache
# and Ninja Training

FACT: mustaches are hilarious. Which is why I collect them. Everything is funnier with a mustache.

At least that's what I hoped. I had a plan, but it was risky.

I overheard Cassie telling Sailor that they were going to talk about the school play at recess. I needed to be in on that conversation. After all, it might start off my amazing career as a comic. Or an actress. Or a comedic actress.

Deep breath.

They might think I was a complete weirdo. Or they might think I was hilarious and let me in on all their plans.

I reached into my pocket and looked down at my choices. The green one? Brown?

Nuh-uh.

Pink? Yeah. Pink, for sure.

Before I could change my mind, I peeled off the thin sheet of paper on the back and slapped the pink strip onto my upper lip.

Sailor happened to glance over at me through her red curls as we walked down the school hallway toward the big doors. Maybe my movement caught her attention. She did a double take. This was it. I wiggled my eyebrows for effect, but on the inside I was holding my breath.

*Please laugh. Please laugh.*

Sailor's eyes widened and then a giggle escaped. The giggle grew into a full-on laugh, which made her curly hair bounce. I broke out into a celebration dance that started out as a little shaky-shaky of happiness and ended in me doing the worm down the hall.

Okay. I didn't actually dance. Part of me wanted to, but the rest of me couldn't quite do it in the hall with everyone watching. Maybe if it was just Sailor, but she wasn't the one I was worried about.

Plus, the worm is really hard.

Hannah looked back too. She didn't laugh enough to show her braces, but her cheeks bobbed. Then Sailor almost snorted. If she had, maybe I really would have danced.

"Oh, hilarious," Yasmin said, quickly reaching into her pocket and pulling out her phone. Was she going to take my picture? No one had ever taken a picture of me at school before. Well, not counting class pictures. I smiled and gave Yasmin a thumbs-up while she clicked the pic. I hoped it looked cute. But she probably didn't have any other photos of a short, twelve-year-old girl with sandy-blonde hair wearing the most beautiful pink mustache a quarter could buy.

I also had a thick green mustache and a curly brown one, but they were still in my pocket. Like I said, everything is funnier with a mustache. For example, think of a pig. They're cute and funny with their piggy snouts and curly pink tails. Now imagine one with a mustache. Yep. Funnier. Or think of a woman in a fancy dress singing opera. Now imagine a mustached woman in a fancy dress singing opera. Think of your baby brother . . . with a mustache.

I almost snorted just thinking about it. But laughing at my own jokes wasn't the best idea, especially jokes I didn't say out loud.

Three of the girls liked my mustache, but I still wanted to win one more girl over. The hardest to impress.

Cassie turned to find out why everyone was laughing and taking pictures. She had been talking to Sarah at the front of the group. Cassie is like the queen of the sixth grade. Well, the queen, the president, the fashionista, winner of the People's Choice Award—pretty much everything important. It isn't official or anything, but everyone knows it.

She wore her blonde hair long and flowy, with a few fancy

braids, the kind moms have to learn how to do by going to beauty school or by watching a lot of videos on the Internet. She also wore a glittery red sweater. Super cute, but we wouldn't expect anything less.

"Maddie! So funny," Cassie said, showing her brilliantly white teeth. "Weird, but funny."

I wanted to pump my fist in the air. The queen thought I was funny. Maybe I could work my way up to becoming the jester of the sixth grade. That would be awesome. My risky risk was paying off. Hopefully, she would let me hang out with her today.

I jogged to catch up to the other girls. All of them were taller than I was, and they seemed to walk faster, too. We opened the big black doors and walked out of Acord Elementary, glad to have at least a few minutes of freedom.

Cassie turned, this time walking completely backwards, looking at the bunch of us following her. She could even walk sassy backwards. "Okay," she said with her big, bright smile, "I need to talk with Sailor, Sarah, and Hannah."

She looked over her shoulder to make sure she was following the walking path around the school. Every recess Cassie picked who got to walk around with her. Sometimes she chose me and we talked about movies and makeup and funny jokes and boys. Well, I didn't usually do much of the talking, but it was still fun.

Some recesses I didn't get picked. Cassie didn't like it if I tried to hang out with a different group, so if I didn't get picked, I usually chilled by the door and made up jokes to myself or invented crazy stories. Once I made up one about a cyclops who had to go on a treacherous journey to get the only contact lens big enough for his monster eye. It was pretty awesome. Well, as awesome as telling a story to yourself can be.

"And Yasmin," Cassie said.

I liked Yasmin and was glad Cassie picked her. And not just because she took a picture of me with her phone. Yasmin and I walked most of the way home together every day. She lived a street over. She had really dark, straight hair and dark skin. She once told me to guess where she was from. I guessed India. I was so wrong. It was Ohio. But her grandparents were from Malaysia. That's somewhere way across the ocean. I could point it out on a map, I think.

"And . . ." Cassie said.

This was it.

*Please. Please.*

I hoped my mustache sealed it. "Definitely Maddie." Phew. I almost danced for real. Not only was I in, but I got a *definitely.* Behold the power of the mustache. "Even though she's holding her arm weird again," Cassie added.

For the love of potatoes! I had forgotten about my arm. I stretched it out quick and hoped my face didn't turn too red. For some reason my arm liked to rest in a funny position sometimes. Cassie had pointed it out three times over the last few days. My fist would tuck in close to my chest and my elbow would stick out behind it. It was probably because I was grow-ing. Bodies do weird things when they grow. At least that's what they told us in that super awkward presentation at school. You know, that one your parents have to sign the permission slip for you to go to and where they talk about deodorant and your body changing. The permission slip probably asked, "Is it okay for your son or daughter to sit through the most embarrassing presentation of their lives?" And all the parents signed it.

Or maybe I held my arm weird because of the ninja train-ing I was doing after school in the invisible dojo in my base-ment. That was probably it. I was almost a titanium belt. That's like twenty levels above black, and it's when you learn to break cars with your pinky finger and bust through freeways with your head. Yeah. That kind of training is intense.

Okay, I made up the ninja stuff, but it sounded pretty cool. Anyway, I straightened my arm. At least Cassie had still picked me.

But Cassie wasn't looking at me anymore. She looked at Lexi, the last girl not picked. She had only been in our school since the end of November, and now it was January, but she seemed nice enough. She looked at us through her brown hair.

"Sorry," Cassie said. She smiled nice and big, but I don't think she was smiling on the inside.

I had seen that same smile lots of times. Like all the times when she told me she was sorry but I couldn't walk with her.

I really didn't like that kind of smile. It was like it was painted on.

I took another deep breath. A thought was pounding on my brain, but I wasn't sure I should say it. I had risked a lot for this. "Wait," I finally said. And then everyone looked at me.

Gulp.

I glanced at Lexi. She was nice and probably hated being alone for recess just as much as I did. "Let's let Lexi hang out with us, too."

Silence.

Nobody said stuff like that. Cassie was in charge. Kelsi said something like that to Cassie once last year and hasn't been invited back since.

"Seriously," I said, finding some courage somewhere deep inside me. "I don't think it's fair to invite all of us and then leave her out. Plus, she's new."

Something about that felt really good. Well, it would have if I had actually done it. I wanted to, but I didn't do it. I only imagined it. Just like my celebration dance and my ninja training.

Maybe I could suggest that . . . No. Cassie might kick me out of the group. Just because I made everyone laugh with my mustache didn't mean they wouldn't drop me. And then I wouldn't be in on the plans about the play. And maybe, just maybe, my comic-actress career would be over before it even started.

I felt bad for Lexi, but I didn't say anything. I was just glad it wasn't me.

# CHAPTER 2

# Poison-tipped Swords, Yelling Matches, and Juliet

"Okay, girls," Cassie said, leading us down the blacktop path around the school fields and away from Lexi. When we were younger, we played four square or tetherball or tag at recess, but not anymore. Cassie said that she was more mature and just wanted to talk.

"We need to talk about the plays," Cassie continued. Her eyes grew bigger, and she smiled wide. Everything was more exciting when Cassie talked about it. "I just know they're going to be amazing this year."

We all agreed. Almost every sixth grader looked forward to the Shakespeare unit in school. Not because we were super fancy-pants kids, because we weren't—well, Cassie wore some pretty fancy pants, but that's not the same thing. We looked forward to the plays because we got to spend a month pretending and getting ready to put on a show.

A real show too. Not a cheesy program. Each class did scenes from different plays. They were short, a couple of minutes long, but they had sword fights and yelling matches and funny bits. And we did it during the day for the whole school and then at night for our parents. I watched it year after year, picking the different parts I would want.

We'd already studied the plots of each play we could choose from, and Mrs. Baer talked about the characters we could pick. We were going to fill out our papers with our top three choices right after recess.

Cassie surveyed all of us and then looked at Hannah. "I think Hannah should be that fairy queen," she said. "So definitely put that down as your first choice."

Hannah nodded. "I would love that." The fairy queen was in *A Midsummer Night's Dream*. That sounded like a pretty fantastic part, but I wasn't sure Hannah remembered what happened in the play. The fairy queen has a spell put on her and falls in love with a guy with a donkey head. Yep. A donkey head. Hilarious, right? The only thing better would be a guy with a donkey head and a mustache.

I choked down a laugh just thinking about it. But it would have been pretty funny if my *he-he-he* would have slipped out as a *he-haw-he*. Get it? Donkey head. He-*haw*-he. Yeah, Cassie probably wouldn't have thought it was funny either. Good thing I kept that one to myself.

"In fact," Cassie said, "you might want to put the fairy queen down for all three choices. Then they'll know you *really* want it." Cassie turned to the rest of us. "No one else put the fairy queen down as one of your three choices, that way Hannah will definitely get it." Everyone agreed, but Sailor nodded slower.

I wanted to ask her if she wanted the part, but everyone was still listening to Cassie.

"And Yasmin," Cassie said. "What should you be?"

"Hero," Sarah suggested.

Yep, there was a girl named Hero in one of the plays. But her name was seriously misleading; she wasn't actually a hero. She didn't sword fight a bad guy, or lead soldiers into war, or use magic to turn the villain's noggin into a donkey's head with a mustache. She just looked pretty and was nice and a guy fell in love with her. And when he was being a jerk, she pretended to be dead. That was it. Again, not really much of a hero.

"I was thinking of auditioning for Juliet," Yasmin said. I could tell from her eyes and bouncy walk that she was pretty excited about that part. A lot of the girls wanted to be Juliet. When the community theater closed down a few years ago, they gave the school a bunch of costumes. Juliet's was the best costume, and super pretty. A light-blue dress, long and flowy, with puffy sleeves and a big sparkly necklace. Plus, she was the most famous part of all of Shakespeare's plays. Everyone's heard of her. Her lines were kinda lovey, and she didn't say much that was funny, but it would still be really fun.

"No," Cassie said, shaking her head. "I don't think Juliet's right for you. What about the nice sister in *Taming of the Shrew*? Bianca. She's pretty and that one boy super wants to marry her."

That part would be okay, but it wasn't Juliet.

"Why don't you think Yasmin should be Juliet?" I asked. "I think it's a great idea." I did think it would be a great idea. Yasmin was smart and could memorize her lines. Plus, she was probably good on stage. I mean, she was pretty fun when we walked home together.

But, like with Lexi, I didn't really ask even though I thought maybe I should. I don't know why. Sometimes I don't say what I think I should.

One by one, Cassie went through the group, giving advice on what to write down. Sailor wanted Juliet too, but Cassie didn't think it was right for her, either. We were passing the school again. We had walked around once and were starting our second time. I saw Lexi sitting alone against the doors to the school, waiting for recess to be over.

My heart flopped a little. Been there. Lots of times.

I wished I would have said something about Lexi. Of course it wouldn't have done much good. Cassie didn't always include everyone, but we all liked her, and she really could be nice. She was just picky sometimes.

"Maddie," Cassie said. "Do you know what part would be great for you?"

I took another deep breath. I had an idea, and I thought I'd try it. "All I care about is that I get to rock a mustache," I said and raised my pink mustache to my lip. I had been thinking up that line for the last half lap.

I don't know why I could talk about mustaches but not ask if Lexi could join us or if Yasmin could be Juliet. They were just different.

Thankfully, everyone laughed again.

Well, everyone except Cassie.

"I like it," Yasmin said. "Maybe Hamlet. He gets to do an awesome sword fight with poison-tipped swords."

"You could be the fairy king," Sailor said.

"No," Cassie said. "Maddie can't be a boy in the play."

I wanted to disagree. We learned that in Shakespeare's day, boys used to play the girls' parts, so it would only be fair if I could put on a mustache and play a boy's part.

"I think you should be Juliet's nurse," Cassie said. "Then we could be together."

The nurse? I didn't want to be the nurse. The nurse was a funny enough character in the real play, but she was only in one of the two *Romeo and Juliet* scenes we were doing, and she only had two or three lines. And they weren't even good. She just kept calling for Juliet to come inside and stop flirting. Of course she said it all Shakespeare-style, like "Forsooth, Juliet, get thine self backeth inside thine house. Thou art boy-crazy."

Okay, maybe I made up that bit.

Wait. What had Cassie said? Then we'd be together? Why would we be . . . ? My brain finally figured it out. Cassie wanted to be Juliet. Was that why she was recommending what everyone else should write down? Was she trying to make it more likely that she would get the part she wanted? No. She was probably just being helpful.

"Maybe the nurse would be okay," I said. Why did I say that? I didn't want to be the nurse. Then again, it *would* be fun to be in a scene with Cassie. With the way she moved and talked, always drawing everyone's attention, it would probably be the best scene of all of them.

Cassie pulled her sparkly pink phone from her pocket. Not only was it cute, but it was one of the newest, fastest phones out there. "The bell is about to ring." I guess she had checked the time. "Let's run in and fill out our papers. I bet if we turn them in first, we get first choice."

All the girls ran. Cassie was in the front, her hair bouncing as she moved.

I ran too but couldn't keep up. I was the slowest and the trippiest of probably everyone in my grade. Maybe I was so clumsy because my legs were growing. I think the teacher might have mentioned that in the awkward class. Or maybe I was really a centaur from some fantasyland, but I was cursed to stay in a human form because I was the princess centaur destined to overthrow the maniacal wizard who had a face like a boar and who had taken over my world. Since I'd been in human form for so long, my legs were getting a little slow.

Yep. Centaur legs don't like being human legs for long. It was kind of like my left hand. I just hoped I could remove the curse soon, because if my clumsiness started to bother Cassie like my arm did, maybe I wouldn't get picked anymore—even with my mustaches. Then I might end up like Lexi again, alone during recess.

I was the last of the girls to get into the classroom. Cassie and the others gathered by the in-box on Mrs. Baer's desk to turn in their preferences. I looked at my paper. I wanted to quickly write down "Hamlet," "Katherine," and "Juliet," but that would mess things up.

"Can I see what you wrote?" I heard Cassie ask Hannah before she dropped her paper in the box.

"Fairy Queen for all three," Hannah said, showing Cassie her paper.

Cassie celebrated and gave Hannah a hug.

Oh, no. My insides rolled. Cassie was probably going to ask to see my paper too. I quickly scribbled down three names:

1. Juliet's nurse
2. Katherine
3. Hamlet

I didn't put Juliet's nurse for all three, but if I put it at number one, I'd get it. I doubt anyone else was trying to get that part.

I didn't even wait for Cassie to ask. I showed my paper to her as soon as I walked over to Mrs. Baer's desk.

She beamed. "I'm so excited," she said. "It's going to be fantastic." She passed me as she went back to her seat. She had already dropped her paper of her top three choices in the box.

I looked at my sheet again. It would be fun to be in a scene with Cassie, but . . . I wrinkled the corner of the paper and looked around the room. Lexi had finished her list and was walking back to her desk. She saw me, and then looked to the floor.

I glanced back at Cassie. She was happily talking with Devin and flipping her hair. I took out my pencil and erased part of my first answer. Now it only said "Juliet" for my first choice.

I didn't just imagine it. I really did it. *And* I turned it in.

# CHAPTER 3

—•—

# Nothing to Worry About

"This Halloween I want to be Frankenstein so I can eat people's brains," Emery, one of my twin brothers, said. Yep, twin brothers. Emery and Ethan are eight, and identical. Have you ever noticed how many twins in movies are evil troublemakers? Well, there's a reason. My brothers are crazy and probably evil.

I'm just kidding. Kind of.

"Frankenstein doesn't eat brains," Ethan said. "That's zombies." They both have high-pitched voices and speak really fast. They kind of sound like hyper chipmunks. Evil hyper chipmunks.

"Oh, yeah," Emery admitted.

"Unless it's a zombie Frankenstein," Ethan said, rising out of his chair, his eyes wide. He pushed aside the plate of meat loaf and potatoes in front of him for a moment.

"Awesome. I'm so glad I thought of it."

"No, you didn't. I did."

"Boys," my mom said, her voice raised to be heard above the chipmunk chatter. "Eat your dinner and stop talking about the undead at the table. It's gross." She had a point. Plus we were eating ground beef.

My mom's fun, funny, and looks young for her age. My dad says she has a baby face, but that's stupid. Can you imagine a full-grown mom with a baby's face? Weird.

I took a bite of my baked potato. I think we can probably all agree that potatoes are the best food ever. They should be an essential part of every meal. It's like they are sent straight from heaven by angels with amazing taste buds. Mashed, baked, French fried, and even sweet potatoes . . . I love them all.

They were especially good after going against Cassie's orders and putting down that I wanted Juliet. I kind of felt bad, and I kind of didn't. And it made me hope that I really could get Juliet, but also terrified that I would.

I took another bite of potato, ignoring my meat loaf. I hate meat. It's the worst food group ever. Nasty. I don't like the idea of killing any animals, especially cows. Cows are cute. But I loved the idea of putting mustaches on cows and watching them chew grass really slowly.

So funny. Cow'staches.

"Yeah, let's worry about Halloween later," my dad said. "It's eight months away." My dad is bald. That's the most important thing to know about him. Well, it's the most obvious thing anyway. If you saw him, you'd want to rub his head for luck.

He's also a writer. He writes curriculum for schools, but on the side, he's been trying to get a book published for years. He's written several stories and sent them to lots of places, and he finally got a deal for his first book. I think it's pretty awesome, but he still has a few months before it comes out. He's even going to go on a tour to promote it.

I love my dad's stories. I love that we share the same kind of imagination. Telling stories and making up stuff is one of my favorite things to do with my dad.

Dad glanced at my plate. "Maddie, eat your meat loaf."

I shuddered. "Meat is disgusting."

"You're being ridiculous," my dad said.

"Yeah, you're being widiculous," Max, my littlest brother, said, smiling big. He's the only one in our family with red hair, and he's the youngest. Three years old. Plus he's adorable.

"If 'ridiculous' means 'awesome,' then yes," I said. "I'm being ridiculous."

My parents laughed. It wasn't fake laughing either. I hear adults do that a lot when kids try to be funny. But I could make my parents laugh, a really real laugh, from the belly.

"Nice job, my little comedian," Mom said, then pointed at my plate. "Now, eat your meat loaf."

That didn't make me laugh.

At all.

"Dad?" Ethan asked. "When does your book come out?"

"You ask that all the time," Christopher said.

Yep, that's another brother—and the oldest. And you counted right. I have four brothers. Four. And no sisters. So my house was crazy and full of boys and boy stuff like soccer balls, dragon movies, and really stinky socks. And if you didn't know, boys' feet stink a lot more than girls' feet. I'm sure science has proved that somewhere.

"It's on March fourth," Christopher said. He loved books. He spent most of his time reading, writing, or playing his trombone. Sometimes all at the same time. Just kidding. That would be really hard.

"I just forget," Ethan said.

"I didn't," Emery said.

"Yes, you did."

"No, I didn't." It was a high-pitched twin argument.

"Boys, calm down," Mom said.

"You've got a problem with your brain," Ethan snapped.

They could go from joking to upset really quickly.

"You've got a problem with your *face*," Emery shot back. "Ugly face." He fake-punched his twin. They weren't supposed to hit each other, so that was the way they showed they were really mad. I knew what was going to happen next. They'd start yelling and both would end up in time-out. That wasn't all bad. Then I could eat my potatoes in peace.

But that didn't happen.

My dad burst out laughing.

Everyone looked at him. Usually he would reprimand the twins for saying mean things to each other, not crack up.

Dad opened his mouth to say something but had to wait a few seconds before he could get the words out. "You said he had an ugly face," he said. I still didn't get why that was funny. He laughed a little more. "But you're identical twins." There was another pause. "You have the *same* face."

Laughter bubbled out of me. I mean, I got the full-on giggles until I noticed my mom looking at me.

"Maddie," she said. "You're holding your arm a little strange again. Are you sure it's alright?"

I looked down at my arm. "Oh, sorry. It just feels comfortable like this. I think it's fine." I stretched my arm out straight to show her it was okay. They had asked about it before, and I'd convinced them it was because I was growing. I didn't want to mention that I'd noticed my hand was different. A little slower to move. It was probably going to get better soon.

Dad was looking at it too. "I think we need to check it out."

"I agree," Mom said. "I'll make an appointment with the doctor."

"It feels fine," I said. Okay, maybe I didn't tell the whole truth, but I didn't like all the questions. Plus, I didn't want to go to the doctor. Going to the doctor meant that something was wrong with you. I wasn't sick. I didn't cough and lay in bed all day. I was fine. And instead of talking about all this stuff, I'd rather just eat potatoes, hope everything would go well with my Shakespeare part, and pray my dad wouldn't actually make me eat my meat loaf.

"I'm glad," Mom said. "But I'm still calling the doctor."

# CHAPTER 4

# Sneezing Laser Beams?

"Romeo. Romeo. Wherefore art thou *Romeo*?" Cassie asked no one in particular. Yasmin, Cassie, and I were in line with a string of other students to audition for our parts, and apparently Cassie was auditioning a little early. The other girls— Sarah, Hannah, and Sailor—were with the other half of the class in computer time with Mrs. Larkin. They would audition after us when it was our turn on the computers.

"Wherefore art *thou* Romeo," Cassie repeated. This time she put the emphasis on the word *thou* instead of *Romeo*. She sounded pretty professional.

Even though Mrs. Baer had already explained that in this

case *wherefore* meant *why* and not *where*, I had an idea for a joke. I gave it a shot.

"Maybe Romeo's right there," I said. I started to extend my arm to point, but it didn't want to move. Weird arm. I quickly used my other arm to point at Cesar. He was the first boy I saw, standing next to Devin, his best friend.

Cassie looked where I was pointing. Yasmin looked at Cassie. "Are you blushing?"

"No," Cassie said. "I'm not."

But she did kind of look like she was turning red. She didn't do that very often. "Are you sure?" I asked. I didn't want to make her uncomfortable, but this was pretty fun, and her cheeks were a little rosy.

"I did not blush," Cassie insisted in a *that's-final* tone. "And you're holding your arm funny again, Maddie."

I looked down. It had slipped back. Maybe *I* was turning a little red now. My doctor visit wasn't until next week. I guess it was hard to find a time that would work between the doctor's schedule and my mom's. And my hand was getting a little harder to open. "It's probably because of my ninja training," I said.

Yasmin laughed.

Cassie didn't.

Maybe I shouldn't have tried my joke.

The door to the small room ahead of us opened. "Great job, Jack," Mrs. Baer said, her hand on the doorknob. Jack walked out and looked like he had just escaped a torture chamber. Apparently, he wasn't as excited as we were about the play.

"Okay, who's next?" Mrs. Baer looked back at the line. "Come on in, Cassie." I could see Mrs. West inside the room writing notes on a clipboard. She was the music teacher and was helping Mrs. Baer cast the parts. Cassie walked in her very best Juliet walk.

Yasmin waited for them to enter the room and close the door before she leaned toward me. "I think she blushed," she said.

"Definitely," I agreed. I hoped it wouldn't bother Cassie that we teased her and she'd still let us hang out with her at recess.

Yasmin looked at the closed door for a moment and played with her fingers. "I'm way nervous," she said.

"Me too," I admitted. My palms were getting sweaty.

"You are?" Yasmin asked. "You're great in front of people."

Really? She thought that? I was usually pretty terrified when everyone was watching me.

"I'm not like that," she said. "I'm practically shaking."

"Oh, I'm not very good in front of people," I said. "But you'll do great," I was already feeling calmer. With Cassie gone and me just hanging out with Yasmin, I felt a lot of the pressure fade away. But I didn't want to think about being nervous for my audition or what part I might get. Or about how my arm was being weird again. We both could use a distraction.

"What if you could pick between being superstrong or being able to fly?" I asked Yasmin.

Yasmin smiled. "That's random."

"Just answer," I said.

"I'm not sure," she said. "I haven't thought about it." She squinched her eyebrows a little. "How about you?"

"I think I'd fly," I said. "Because really, how much am I going to have to lift?"

"Good point," Yasmin said. "But then if Coby teased you like he teases some of the other kids, you could punch him into the Pacific Ocean."

"Oh, that's tempting," I said, laughing between words. "But if I could fly, I could just pick him up and drop him in the Pacific Ocean. Or even better, the Arctic Ocean. Then he'd be a Cobysicle. Plus every morning I could sleep in ten more minutes and then just shoot over to school and not be late."

"Good call," Yasmin agreed. I think we were both feeling a lot better.

"What if you were surrounded by bad guys," I said, "and you had to pick between being able to sneeze laser beams or burp bombs?"

Yasmin giggled.

"Burp bombs?" Devin said. Apparently the two girls behind us had left the line and he and Cesar had stepped up.

Oh no. They were listening? To that? What was I going to say? The question repeated like three hundred times in my head in less than a second. Finally, my mouth blurted something out. "You'd burp bombs?" I asked.

"No." He laughed. "I don't want to burp bombs. I was just making sure I heard you right."

"And that was a bizarre question," Cesar said.

I'm sure my face was getting hotter, but I didn't want it to. I don't know why I was getting nervous. I'd known Devin and Cesar for years. "Well, choose wisely," I said. I was talking more and more. Nervous, remember? "You have to pick that or sneezing lasers. It's an important decision."

"It is a toughy," Yasmin said.

"I think it sounds cooler to sneeze lasers," Devin said. "But then I probably couldn't control them very well. Everybody's head moves all around when they sneeze." He did a fake sneeze for a demonstration. He was right. Lasers would go everywhere.

"But I can burp whenever I want," Cesar said. And then he burped. Loud.

I didn't know whether to laugh or say "Eww." So I kind of did both.

Cesar probably wouldn't make the best Romeo.

"Whoa," Devin said. "Maybe you can already burp bombs."

We all laughed at that.

And then the door opened, and I turned to see Cassie walk out of her audition. "How did it go?" I asked.

"Great," she said, all teeth and smiles. "Really great." But she didn't look at me or Yasmin. It was like she stared through us at Cesar and Devin. I guess Juliet was so interested in Romeo she didn't want to be bothered with the nurse.

She probably hadn't just heard Cesar belch.

"Maddie," Mrs. Baer said. "Come on in."

I took in a quick breath.

"Good luck," Yasmin said and gave me a hug.

"Thanks," I said as I walked through the doorway and toward a little opening between the rows of desks. Still wrapped up with the boys, Cassie didn't wish me luck. She didn't even look back at me.

Mrs. West sat in a desk at the front of the room and was writing more notes, probably from Cassie's audition. She didn't look up. She probably had a lot of really good stuff to write.

"Okay," Mrs. Baer said, looking at a clipboard as she sat down next to Mrs. West. "Just relax and do your best." She looked up with a smile, the super nice kind that made me more relaxed. She flipped over a page. "It looks like you wanted to try out for Hamlet, Kate, and Juliet." She extended her arm as if to say the stage was mine, but there wasn't actually a stage. Just a mostly empty room. "Go ahead."

And that was it. There were no warm-ups, just "Go ahead." I don't know what I was expecting, but it wasn't just jumping in. I looked at the teachers. Awkward. Have you ever tried to act in front of two people? Not just playing around with your friends, but like people who *want* you to act? I'd always wanted to be in plays, but this felt strange.

I opened my mouth to start, but nothing came out. "Uh." I couldn't remember my words. It was like they were on a little computer screen in my mind and then I accidentally turned it all off and now I had to wait for the thing to reboot. But I had to say something. "Hark, fair ladies," I said. "I believe I've forgotten my lines."

They both smiled back. That relaxed me even more. So I decided to reach into my pocket and pull out a mustache. I put it on and wiggled my eyebrows.

Two more smiles. Maybe this wouldn't be that bad. And maybe fake mustaches were the best invention ever.

I cleared my throat and stretched out my weird arm. The computer in my brain turned back on.

"Alas, poor Yorick! I knew him well." I pretended to hold a skull in my hands. Yep, that's what happens in the play; Hamlet speaks to a skull. Weird and awesome. I rattled out a few more Hamlet lines then tore my mustache off.

And then I glared like I was really mad at someone. No. Like I was furious. That's what Kate does. "If I be waspish, best . . . beware . . . my . . . sting." I gave a little space between each word to make it more dramatic. And then on the last word I jumped forward. It wasn't a very big jump because of my tricky leg, but both teachers were startled. Not bad. Maybe audition-ing could actually be fun.

After a few more lines, Mrs. Baer spoke up. "Very good, Maddie." And from the way she said it, I thought she meant it. "And Juliet?" Both she and Mrs. West leaned forward.

I put my hand to my heart and tried to act a little lovey, but not too much. I spoke to the podium in the room like it was Romeo. It didn't give me much to go on, but at least it didn't laugh at me. I said a few lines. They came out easy, like I was supposed to say them. I guess I had really warmed up. I finished with "a thousand times"—I paused for effect—"good night." And then I turned and bowed to the teachers.

Both of them clapped and then whispered to each other. I hoped they were talking about giving me the chance to stab someone with a poisoned sword. Well, not a real poisoned sword, that would be weird if they were talking about that. But, you know—Hamlet.

"Thank you very much, Maddie," Mrs. West said. Those were the first words she had said the whole time. Mrs. Baer thanked me, too, and brought me to the door. They had to keep the auditions moving pretty fast to get through all the students.

"Before I go," I said, now nervous for a completely different reason. "I don't know about being Juliet. I really think Cassie wants to be her."

"It's okay if more than one person wants a part," Mrs. Baer said. "We'll make the choice from here."

"But—"

"Don't worry," she said and escorted me right out of the room.

I had no idea if I was going to be a prince, an angry woman, or Juliet. Well, I could be anything. But if I somehow ended up as Juliet, I didn't know what I would say to Cassie.

# CHAPTER 5

# Dragoporkisaur

"I'm sure it wasn't that bad," I said, stepping beside Yasmin. We were walking the last few blocks home together before she turned down her street.

"No. It was," Yasmin said. "I choked. Completely choked." She pulled out her phone and moved it around with her fingers, not even turning it on. She did that while she was thinking sometimes. I wish I had a phone, but my parents say I can't have one until I'm fourteen. I'm not sure if they are serious, but they don't seem to be planning on getting me one anytime soon.

"If you completely choked, then you would be dead," I said. "Suffocated in your audition." I looked over at her.

Maybe there was a hint of a smile. "And you look pretty alive to me."

"Yeah, I'm alive. But barely," Yasmin said, all exasperated. "I messed up every line."

"I almost forgot *all* of mine," I said.

"Really?"

"Yep." I told Yasmin about the whole thing.

"I wish I'd had a mustache," Yasmin said. "Maybe that would have helped me not be nervous."

I reached into my pocket and pulled out a few. "Here, pick one."

She looked down at my open hand and then back at me. "Are you sure?"

"Yeah," I said. "I have lots. That way if you freeze up on something else, you can just put on a mustache."

"That's awesome," Yasmin said, checking out her choices. "Um, I think I'll pick this one." She nabbed a blue mustache.

"Good choice," I said.

As she held it to her face and turned to me with a smile, something behind us must have caught her eye. She slowed down and looked over my shoulder.

I looked back to see what she was looking at.

Devin and his younger brother, Sam, were walking behind us. They both had dark hair, dark eyebrows, and a cool walk. They seriously looked like the same person, just one was bigger than the other. Like Sam was a clone of Devin. Maybe he was.

That'd be cool since Devin wasn't ugly. It wasn't like I thought he was super good-looking, I was just . . . Oh, never mind.

"Are you checking out Devin?" I asked and bobbed my eyebrows.

"No," Yasmin said, shaking her head. "Behind him." She pointed.

I looked past the two boys and saw a girl with blonde hair in long fancy braids wearing a black shirt with silver stars. "Is that Cassie?" I asked.

"I think so," Yasmin said.

"But why is she walking this way?" Cassie didn't live in the same neighborhood we did, so she didn't usually walk in the same direction as us. In fact, she usually took the bus to her fancy-pantsy neighborhood on the other side of the school.

"No idea," Yasmin said.

"She's walking with Hannah," I said. "Maybe they're hanging out today." Hannah did live close to our neighborhood, but she usually didn't walk with us either.

"Let's wait up for her," Yasmin said. "I mean 'them.'"

I thought that was a good idea so we stood along the sidewalk to let Devin and his brother pass. I noticed my arm was tucked back weird against my side again so I pulled it out.

"Hey, Maddie. Hey, Yasmin," Devin said. That was nice. A lot of boys our age wouldn't even say hi. We both waved back.

"Are those your girlfriends?" Sam asked, even though he knew who I was. I'd been neighbors with Devin and Sam for a long time. They live on my street. Our families have even had barbeques together.

"No," Devin said and whapped his brother on the top of the head. But Devin did turn a little red. I wasn't sure if it was because he liked one of us or if he was embarrassed because his brother was talking about girlfriends.

The fact that he blushed at all made me tense. I had to say something. "No," I said to Devin's little brother as he walked by. "I'm *your* girlfriend, Sam."

"No, you're not," Sam said and stuck out his tongue. He was in the first grade so it was adorable. Devin laughed, and they kept walking.

Then Cassie passed with Hannah. Both Yasmin and I waved and said hi as we started to walk with them.

But they didn't wave back. Well, Cassie tilted her head a little.

"I hope it's me," Cassie said.

"But you didn't hear for sure?" Hannah asked. Cassie shook her head. "He'd be crazy if it isn't you."

"Thanks," Cassie said.

They hadn't really acknowledged us, but they were deep in conversation. We walked for a little while longer before I dared joining in. "What are you talking about?" I asked. At first I thought it might be the auditions, but they had mentioned a *he*. Both the teachers who were casting were *shes*.

Cassie and Hannah just kept talking, like I hadn't said anything at all.

Weird.

Yasmin and I shared a look.

Really? It was even worse than when Cassie came out of her auditions.

We slowed our walk. Then slower. Hannah and Cassie moved farther and farther ahead of us, not even noticing.

It was like we weren't even there. Yasmin and I shared another look. Why would they do that?

"Oh, no," I said, glancing down.

"What?" Yasmin asked.

"I know why they couldn't see us. I'm being summoned."

"What are you talking about?"

"I'm part of this interdimensional super-fighter team that keeps all sorts of worlds and universes from getting destroyed and stuff," I explained. I thought about doing a karate kick to prove my point but decided against it. My leg was feeling trippy. "And one of my team members is pulling me out of our dimension and into another. I've been disappearing for the last two minutes. Probably right after Devin and Sam saw us. And because you're next to me, you're disappearing too."

Yasmin looked at me strangely, but a smile hid in the corner of her mouth.

"Seriously, I can barely even see you," I said. "And any

minute we'll be in another place entirely. Be ready. We don't know what we're about to face."

Yasmin let out a happy gasp. "You're so weird."

And then just like that, we were in another world. It was like we faded in. The rows of houses around us turned into huge mountains reaching up into a dark sky, but instead of cars and mailboxes, there were hundreds of people screaming in panic and running for their lives. And they weren't like normal people. They wore clothes made out of animal skins, and everyone's hair was all messy, poking out in every direction. Then I saw why they were running.

"Oh, no!" I said, looking up, then quickly winking at Yasmin to play along. "Not him again. My mortal enemy." My worst nightmare loomed above us, about five schools tall with a head as big as Mrs. Baer's classroom.

"What is it?" Yasmin asked, winking back, then gazing up. She obviously had never seen one before.

"One of the most feared beasts in the universe—Dragoporkisaur," I explained. "Part dragon. Part dinosaur. And a lot pig."

Yasmin nearly snorted. "That's gonna be a problem."

"You have no idea," I said. "Quick, behind that wall!" We both moved moments before a barrage of fire from the beast would have burned us to crispy critters.

"That was close," Yasmin said.

"Yep," I said. Even my slow leg moved faster when

Dragoporkisaur was on my trail. A whiff of smoke curled up into my nostrils. "Ew," I said, waving my hand in front of my face. "After the fire, you can always smell the dragon-piggy breath. Disgusting."

Yasmin crinkled her nose.

"Whoa," I said as the ground started to wobble. "The monster's huge pig snort is causing an earthquake."

Yasmin shook with me, the ground lurching beneath our feet. "How come you're not like this at school?" she asked.

"I am. It's just I'm teleported into other dimensions so you don't notice," I said.

"Well," Yasmin said, "it's totally fun."

"I just hope he doesn't try to smash us with his curly, spiked tail," I said, pointing it out to Yasmin. I took a deep breath. It was that hero moment you see in movies. The time of decision. "I'm going to have to face him." I tried to stretch out my arm to get ready for our battle, but it didn't move nearly as well as usual. Not good, but I was still going to have to square off against the beast.

"How do you defeat something like this?" Yasmin asked.

"Easy," I said. "I can sneeze laser beams."

Yasmin smiled big. "And I burp bombs. I'll come with you."

"Alright," I said. "Tonight you're going to have the biggest slices of bacon you've ever seen."

We both charged out from behind the wall.

# CHAPTER 6

## A Flying Avocado

Guacamole.

Yum.

It's fun to say: guacamole. Try it. *Guacamole.*

My mom and I had some time before school, and we were making guacamole. I really liked to help my mom in the kitchen, mostly because at the end, I got to eat something delicious.

"Catch," Mom said, and threw me an avocado. Even though the avocado was gliding toward my left side, I tried to catch it with my right hand. That didn't work out so well. It hit my shoulder and fell to the floor.

Not good. If it hit the ground too hard, we'd have guacamole on the floor.

My mom looked at me for a moment then down to my left hand. It hadn't moved. "Why didn't you use both hands, Maddie?"

I shrugged. "I don't know."

My mom stepped closer. Her eyes turned more serious. "Maddie, yes, you do. Has it gotten worse?" She pointed to my left arm.

I didn't want to tell her. It probably wasn't a big deal. No use worrying anyone. It had been four days since my mom made the doctor's appointment, and that still wasn't until next week. The doctor would know.

But my mom gave me the "I'm not backing down on this question" look. There was no way out. "It doesn't really work well." The words felt weird coming out of my mouth.

Mom tilted her head as she looked at me. "What do you mean?"

I extended my arm out from its place at my side and opened my hand. It shook a little as I moved it. "It really wants to be closed."

"Can you do this?" Mom opened and closed her hand quickly.

I tried to do the same, but it took a lot of concentration and I was slow. It may have even been slower than a few days ago.

"How about the other hand?" Mom pointed to my right hand.

I opened and shut that one just fine. "It's just the left one."

"Is it this way all the time?" Mom asked and grabbed my left arm to look it over.

"Pretty much."

"Does anything else feel strange?"

"Well, my toes curl up and make me trip sometimes."

"Which foot?" Mom had a lot of questions.

"My left one," I answered.

"Smile for me." She leaned down to get a good view of my mouth.

What did my smile have to do with anything? I smiled anyway. Mom asked me to, and I'm supposed to do what my mom says. Plus, she's one of my best friends in the world. I'm sure my smile was weird. You try to smile when someone just asks you to. Of course, if I was wearing a mustache it would have looked awesome.

Mom wasn't done. She looked things up on her phone and asked me all sorts of questions. She asked if I felt any tingling. She had me follow her finger with my eyes. I think I was passing most of her tests. Finally, she smiled at me, but it was a little bit of a cover-up smile—I could tell. "You go ahead and walk to school with the other kids. I'll call the doctor as soon as he's in the office."

I wondered what she was thinking, but somehow I knew she didn't want to wait until my appointment next week. I hoped nothing was really wrong.

# CHAPTER 7

# Immediately

As far as teachers go, Mrs. Baer rocked. We did all sorts of fun stuff in her class, like spelling games where if you got so many words right you could shoot invading UFOs from the sky. She even had a "Baer Box" filled with candy and posters and stuff for super good behavior. All of Mrs. Baer's room was covered in bears.

Get it? Baer—Bear.

But she didn't cover her room with real bears. That would be terrifying.

"Is today the day we find out what parts we get in the play?" Cassie asked as we stepped into class.

Mrs. Baer clapped her hands. "I know many of you are

very excited about that," she said in her happy-teacher voice. She was good at that. "But no." She shook her head. "It's a lot of work to decide, and we still need another day or two." Several students groaned. "But you'll notice that I changed your seats. Please find your seat and say hello to your new neighbors."

All of our desks were moved around. Maybe I was going to sit next to Yasmin, or Sarah, or even Cassie. That would be awesome. I checked the desks trying to find mine. Out of the corner of my eye, I saw Cassie looking for her desk too. She was easy to find in her sparkly blue T-shirt. It looked like she had already found her seat, so I walked over by her and said hi. "I hope we get to sit together," I said.

"That would be fun," Cassie said. I was really glad to hear her say that after she had ignored me the other day. Maybe we were becoming better friends. Maybe she'd heard that Yasmin and I had destroyed Dragoporkisaur with our laser sneezes and burp bombs. It was pretty impressive after all. "Hey, Maddie," Cassie said. She looked around and then leaned in so only I could hear. "I was wondering if you could do a favor for me?"

"Sure," I said, not thinking twice about it.

Cassie whispered, "Ask Devin who he likes."

Oh. My brain whirred. Either she wanted to know for someone else or Cassie didn't like Cesar—she liked Devin. I didn't think Cassie was trying to find out for someone else. Of course she wouldn't admit to it, but if someone asks that question I think it's pretty obvious. The only thing more obvious would be an "I love Devin" mustache.

I didn't mind talking to Devin, but asking who he liked was different. Really different. Cassie was so pretty and everyone liked her so Devin would probably like her too. It would be weird to ask him and awkward to hear him answer. Then again, maybe it could be like a secret mission. I could sneak in like a spy and find very sensitive information. Yeah, that was a better way of thinking about it. And if I needed a disguise, I had mustaches ready.

"Okay," I said.

"Thanks," Cassie said and flipped her long blonde hair. And it flipped well. Some girls flip their hair and their neck gets all crooked and their hair flip-flops all over the place. I probably did it that way. But Cassie did it like a girl in a movie. Like she'd practiced it hundreds of times. She probably had.

Most kids had found their desks. Every spot on Cassie's row was filled. And on the row behind her. And on the row in front of her. And Yasmin was in the row in front.

Boo. I wasn't going to sit by either of them.

I looked at the few remaining open desks, trying to find mine. They were all on the other side of the room, far away from my friends.

Lexi gave a small wave and motioned for me. I guess my desk was next to hers. That would probably be okay. As I walked over, I saw Devin. He was just a few desks to the side of us. At least I knew someone close. And maybe it would make it easier to find out who he liked.

"Hey, Lexi," I said, immediately feeling bad that Cassie never let her hang out with us. In fact, Cassie hadn't let her hang out with us since that day we talked about which parts to choose. I gave her an "I'm sorry I didn't say anything, but I've been there too" smile. I still felt bad I hadn't stood up for her. I pulled my binder out of my backpack with my good hand.

"Hey, Maddie," she said back.

"How are you?" I asked and put my binder on my desk. Out of the corner of my eye, I saw Devin, and it seemed like he was looking over at us. Did he suspect my secret mission already? Or maybe he was still deciding if he wanted to sneeze lasers beams or burp bombs.

"I'm fine," Lexi said. "Is your arm okay?"

I looked down. "I think so," I said, stretching it out slower than before, but I didn't try to open my hand. I didn't want it to tremble. "It's just been a little weird lately." I wished I could have pulled out my long green mustache from my backpack. If I could have put it on right then, Lexi would have loved it. And it would have distracted her from my arm. Green mustaches are good for that.

Devin. He was still looking toward us.

"Is it just me, or is Devin looking over here a lot?" I asked.

Lexi blushed. Apparently talking about Devin was also a good distraction. Maybe even better than a green mustache.

But not as funny. Now if Devin was wearing a green mustache *that* would have been the best distraction.

"Okay, class," Mrs. Baer said. "Time to get started."

I had to pay attention. In Mrs. Baer's class, if you are good, you can get Baer Bucks. You can also get them for keeping your desk clean or acing a quiz or test. And if you get enough, you could pick something out of the Baer Box. The coupon to "get out of homework for a day" was my favorite.

But we weren't going to do Bear Box for a while. We had a math test. A super long math test.

I think math was invented by some evil organization that was trying to turn all of the human race's brains to mush. And the tragic part was, it probably was working. At least it was probably working on mine.

Static popped out from the speaker above the whiteboard, followed by a beep. "Excuse me, Mrs. Baer," a voice came over the intercom. "Maddie Bridger's mother is here to check her out."

It was weird to hear my name over the intercom. At first I thought I was in trouble, like I was being called down to the principal's office. Maybe they had discovered that I had been tunneling underneath the school and found a huge gold mine miles underground. I had been secretly digging it out and giving the gold to poor families who needed it. I was kind of like Robin Hood but with a hard hat and a pickax.

No. That wasn't it. I was getting checked out of school.

But the only time I got checked out early was on my birthday. My mom checked me out every year and took me to Alfunzo's Fun Zone. We bowled and drove go-carts and played mini-golf and video games. But it definitely wasn't my birthday.

Oh. I knew why.

At least I could leave my math test behind. Take that, dumb evil organization. My brain would not become mush today.

When I reached the office with my pink backpack sagging behind me, I saw my mom with Max standing beside her. I had barely even stepped into the room when Mom hugged me. It was a tight one. "I called the doctor and he said we have to go to the hospital immediately."

*Immediately?*

# CHAPTER 8

# Wrong

"We're going to the doctor," Max blurted out. "Immediately," he repeated.

He was cute in his three-year-old-ness, but hearing the word *immediately* again jarred me.

Still standing in the school's office, I nodded, but I didn't really understand. What was so important that it had to happen immediately? Maybe the doctors needed to see me because they'd found out I'm a cursed centaur ninja with experimental technology in me. And if they didn't find a way to change me back, they'd keep me locked up in the circus where everyone would pay five dollars to see the robot-centaur girl.

I would pay five dollars for that.

But I knew it was because of my arm. Or my leg. Or both. No one would pay five dollars to see those.

We signed out, got in our minivan, and started off.

I'd seen my doctor before for checkups. He was nice and smart and stuff, but the best thing about him was that his name was Ryan Evans. Just like the name of the blond guy in *High School Musical*—Sharpay's twin who wears all the hats. I used to watch that a lot when I was a little kid. Except Dr. Evans wasn't a blond high-school kid who sang and danced while wearing hats. That would have been awesome.

Max waved a stick he must have picked up on the way to the car. "Do you want to play Wizard Club?" He had watched some cartoon about a boy who discovered a magic wand and formed a club of wizards to fight all different kinds of evil creatures. He had been pretending that sticks were wands ever since.

I nodded. I had nothing better to do.

"Do you know which character I want to be?" he asked.

"The most powerful wizard?" I hadn't seen the show, so I didn't know the characters' names, but I'd heard him talk about it.

He shook his head, a wide grin on his face.

"The giant?"

He shook his head again.

"The dragon?"

"Nope. The dwarf," he said.

Really? Out of all of the characters, he picked the dwarf?

"He's short and awesome. Just like me." He pointed at himself with both thumbs.

I was glad I wasn't drinking because if I was, it would have come out my nose. I laughed long and loud. Maybe even extra loud, but it felt good.

While my brother started describing an episode about a stolen pair of magical boots, I looked out the car window. It never took us this long to get to Dr. Evans' office. "Mom, aren't we going too far?"

"No."

"But Dr. Evans' office is . . ."

"Oh, no," my mom interrupted. "We aren't going to Dr. Evans' office. He said we should take you straight to the children's hospital downtown. We still have a ways to go."

A children's hospital? "Why?" I asked.

"Well, they have specialist doctors and better equipment to get pictures of things inside your body."

Something was wrong, and it would take specialists and better equipment to figure it out.

Wrong.

Not ninja training or magic curses.

*Wrong.*

"They probably need a CT scan or an MRI of your brain," my mom said.

I didn't know what those letters meant, but I definitely understood one word. "Brain?"

"Yeah. They just need to make sure it's okay." My mom looked back at me in the rearview mirror. "There's no reason to be worried. We'll have to find out what they see."

No reason to be worried? That's what she said, but I could feel it. It was like worry was a dark cloud that filled our whole van.

"Watch out!" Max called out, waving his wand. I was so tense from what my mom had said that it made me jump. "They've got us surrounded." Apparently he hadn't realized that Mom and I had been talking and this was kind of serious. "You take the ogres. I'll face off with the giant snake."

"Okay," I said. What I really had to face felt worse than squaring off against a bunch of angry ogres.

My brain.

*Something's wrong.*

I wished my little brother could use his wand and just make everything better somehow.

# CHAPTER 9

# Escape Pod

An MRI.

That's what the emergency room doctors said I needed. After three different doctors made me squeeze their hand, kick their palm, follow their finger with my eyes, and smile for them (just like Mom had), they all said they would need to get an MRI scan to know more.

They didn't tell me what the letters in MRI stood for. Massive Robot Intelligence. Mustard Rat from Indiana. Mustaches Rock Importantly. But none of those really made sense, so probably not. The doctors just explained that it would take some fancy pictures of the inside of my head.

Walking to the MRI room wasn't bad, though. There were

kids' paintings on the walls, like one of a dog skiing and another one of a unicorn. Pretty cool. And there were fake fish hanging from the ceiling like they were swimming in the air. Max kept pointing them out.

We walked through a door with a sign that said IMAGING above it. My mom gave the person behind the desk a lot of information about me. She had done that a few times now. It seemed really redundant—that's a word that means something happens over and over again. Or it repeats. Or it happens over and over again.

See what I did there? I think of funny, weird things when I'm nervous. And *redundant* was a vocab word last week.

"Hello, Maddie," a lady in a long white coat said. I wanted her to tell me that everything was going to be okay, that I was just fine. But that was silly. She hadn't even checked me yet. Well, to be honest, I wanted her to tell me that I could go home, that my arm and leg were just growing and I could go back to making my friends laugh with mustaches, hoping for a good part in a Shakespeare scene, and trying to find out who Devin liked. But that wasn't going to happen either.

"Come on back," the lady in the coat said. She led us through the big doors from the waiting area into a wide, medical-looking hall. Tall stands with tubes, beds on wheels, and small portable beeping machines stood outside the doors. We made our way past all of it.

She led us into a room that looked like an office. There was a desk and computers facing a huge window. "Okay, we are going to put you into the MRI machine, and it's going to take pictures of your head, okay?"

I nodded.

"But first you have to take off any jewelry or metal." She was looking me over as she said it.

Usually I'm just dripping in diamonds and gold chains. Oh, and a crown, of course, with emeralds. It's probably worth a quadrillion dollars. Good thing I had left it all with the royal guard back at the palace. That made things easier.

I took out my one pair of earrings with little gold mustaches on them.

"Do you think we'll have to sedate her?" the lady asked my mom.

"She should be fine," Mom said. "She's a brave girl."

I didn't know what *sedate* meant. It wasn't a vocab word last week. But I liked the fact that I was brave. I mean, of course I was brave. I'd put on a mustache at school to make my friends laugh. I'd written that I wanted to be Juliet, even when Cassie wanted me to write something else. I'd defeated an evil mastermind with my remote-controlled spy agents. And when I'd been shrunk to no bigger than a penny, I'd faced the swarm of killer bees by myself to save a colony of ladybugs.

Wait. No. I only did the last two in my imagination.

But I *am* brave.

Just in case, my mom turned to me. "Do you think they

should give you medicine to make you fall asleep while you're in the machine?"

Oh, so that's what *sedate* meant.

"Or can you lie on the table and stay really still?" Mom smiled at me.

I didn't know what machine or table we were talking about, but I nodded. "I can stay still," I said.

The lady in the long coat didn't look convinced. Maybe lots of kids couldn't stay still. That made me wonder if I really could. "Let me show you the machine and you can make sure that's okay," she said. I nodded. "But your mom and your brother will have to stay here."

What? I had to go in alone?

"You'll do great, girl," my mom said and gave me a hug. It was a many-hug day.

"Bye, Maddie," Max said. "You're so lucky." I guess he liked the idea of a machine that could see into my head.

But I didn't feel lucky. I felt alone.

I followed the lady down the hall. This probably wasn't a big deal. I'd had X-rays at the dentist before, and they just put a little machine close to my mouth. I guess that was what I was expecting.

It wasn't even close.

This machine was *huge*.

It practically filled the entire room. It looked like a giant washing machine with a hole in the front. There was just enough room for a person to lie down on a table and slide inside of it. It was like going into a mechanical cave.

The lady confirmed that I was okay to lie there on my own, and then she patted the table, telling me to sit on it.

"Alright," she said. "I just need to give you a shot so the machine can bounce its wave off the medicine in the shot and get a good picture of your insides."

I didn't know what that meant, but I didn't like it. The lady in the coat got a needle. It wasn't tiny. I didn't like that even more. As the needle went in, I felt like I was getting stabbed in the hand with a small sword. My tender, useful hand.

She pushed on the end, and sting-y stuff went into my veins.

I cried.

Call me a wimp, but I had just found out there might be something wrong with my brain, I was going to have to sit in a huge machine, and then I got stabbed with a small sword.

Not my favorite day. Not even close.

The lady waited a minute until I was feeling better, then she laid a thick blanket on top of me. It didn't seem like a blanket though. It was heavy, like it was made of mud and covered in plastic. She strapped my head into a helmet thing that was attached to the table. It probably made me look like a spacewoman.

She also popped some headphones over my ears, but no

music was coming out. They must have been to keep noise out or something.

"Are you okay?" the lady asked.

I was okay. Not good or comfortable or happy, but okay.

"I'm going to put you in the machine as soon as I leave the room," she said.

And then she left.

I was alone.

No Mom.

No Max.

No lady in the lab coat.

Just me in a giant machine.

Really not my favorite day.

The lady must have pushed a button or something because the table suddenly started to move me into the machine. After a few seconds, the top half of my body was surrounded by metal. I could only move a few inches if I wanted to, but I tried to hold super still.

I'd heard that some people get really scared when they are in tight spaces. I wasn't comfortable, but I wasn't terrified. At least, not yet.

"This is going to take a while, Maddie," the lady's voice said over some speakers.

That was twice today I heard my name on an intercom.

"Okay," I said. But I wasn't really okay. They'd put me in some giant machine where I could barely move and left me.

And that's when I realized what was really happening.

*BOOM.*

A burst of fire and torn steel flew into space. Our engine had exploded.

This was it. We were all going to get sucked into the black hole if we didn't act fast.

I jumped into my space suit in under twenty seconds and leaped up onto a small table, pushing the buttons on the control panel above it. A beep sounded, and my whole body moved slowly forward, completely surrounded by metal.

Slowly.

Too slowly.

C'mon. Faster. Faster.

Whoever programed this thing did not think it through. We needed to get into the escape pods quickly. That's why they call them escape pods.

The space suit was too tight, but I knew I'd be glad to have it when I was rocketing toward the next closest planet. Seriously, if you don't have one of these and your escape pod cracks, your blood can boil in less than twenty seconds.

And I didn't want my blood to boil.

Nope.

My escape pod and I needed to get out of reach of the black hole before we imploded. I'm not a big fan of imploding. I can't imagine it feeling very good.

I took a deep breath and let the metal close in around me. Any moment now.

*Beep.*

Please no blood boiling. Please no imploding.

*Beep. Beep. Beep.*

*BRRRRRRRRRRRRRRRRRRRRR.*

I jumped at the noise. It was loud. Really loud. I didn't know what exactly this machine was doing, but it was not doing it quietly. I had the headphones on, and it was still really loud. Seriously, I was under enough pressure as it was without this thing making so much noise.

*Beep. Beep. Beep. BRRRRRRRRRRRRRRRRRRRRR.*

Maybe it was broken or something, but the lady didn't stop it.

No, I had just smacked into a space rock as I rocketed from the ship, trying to escape the inevitable clutches of the black hole. The whole area was filled with space debris.

*BRRRRRRRRRRRRRRRR.*

I bounced against another meteorite.

And another. But after a while, I thought they were getting smaller. I hoped I was getting away from the rocks and closer to safety. The escape pod kept making noise, though. Maybe all the banging and bouncing had done some damage.

More beeps. More brrrrrrrr.

I didn't know shooting into space in an escape pod would

get boring. I was lying there all alone, staying still and listening to the crazy machine booming and ringing and buzzing.

For like forty-five minutes.

Not a very quick escape.

Finally, I was out of reach of the black hole. I just didn't know if I was out of danger.

What had the machine seen when it looked inside my head?

# CHAPTER 10

# Two and a Half Golf Balls

We waited for the doctor a looooooooooooooong time. Maybe it wasn't as long as I thought, but I bet it was. Maybe that *long* needed a few more *O*s. Like, if I was a man, I could have grown a beard in the time we waited. A super long beard. Like a guy in a motorcycle gang would have. Or a dwarf king. Or that guy in the fairy tale who fell asleep for a hundred years. Oh, what was his name? Rip Van Winkle. Yeah. He had a crazy long beard.

I tried to think of anything other than what the MRI might show about my brain. So I wondered about school. I hoped I would get a good Shakespeare part and Cassie wouldn't be upset with me. Oh, and I wondered if Devin liked Cassie like she liked him. I hadn't had a chance to ask him yet.

My dad was sitting with me now. He had been in a meeting when my mom told him the doctor wanted me in the hospital *immediately*. He left right in the middle of his meeting to zoom to the hospital. He got here while I was in the giant metal escape pod. He had a big smile and made lots of jokes. I think he says weird things when he's nervous. I bet that's where I get it.

The hospital had this craft lady who popped into the room to check on me and brought fun stuff, like paints, drawing supplies, and even fingernail polish. I guess if you have to get shots and have doctors test you and put you in a giant machine, they give you stuff to do.

I liked it. I think I'm crafty. That means good at crafts, or it could mean really clever. I'm both. Crafty and crafty. I liked to make bracelets out of beads or rubber bands or crocheted yarn. I'd made bracelets for some of my friends and cousins and Max. They really seemed to like them. Max pretended his was a communicator to talk to Superhero Headquarters.

The craft lady let Max play with the stuff, too. He was making something out of Play-Doh when a doctor came in. She was probably a little older than my mom and wore a blue coat.

"Hello," she said. She was carrying a box of tissues. That was weird. Why would a doctor bring in a box of tissues? Didn't they usually carry bandages and doctor tools?

Oh. Maybe Mom had a booger hanging out of her nose. That would be embarrassing. I checked just to make sure. Nope. My dad didn't either. I did a quick check on my nose, too. I thought I was clean, but I couldn't tell for sure without crossing the room and looking in a mirror. Max had one, though. That's probably why the doctor brought the tissues.

"We have the results back from the MRI," the doctor said. "And Maddie has a brain tumor." She held out the tissue box to my mom.

A tumor. I didn't know what that was—not really.

I looked at my mom and dad. My dad just stared at the doctor. My mom was paying close attention to her, too, but her eyes were different. She didn't cry, but they were different. She waved off the tissues.

The tissues were for wiping away tears. Apparently the doctor thought that the fact I had a tumor should make us cry.

"It's rather large," the doctor said. "About the size of two and a half golf balls."

I didn't really understand what the doctor was saying, but I wanted to pretend that it had something to do with golf. Golf was boring, but mini-golf was fun. And people didn't bring tissue boxes to play mini-golf at Alfunzo's Fun Zone.

"Because it's pushing against her brain, she's having trouble with the left side of her body. It's also right next to the optic nerves and could affect her eyesight, if it hasn't already."

My eyes? I had noticed that my eyes bounced a little sometimes, but only when they were tired.

The doctor kept talking. "The neurosurgery department will be able to answer your questions better than I can. They will likely want to schedule a surgery in a few weeks. It's likely a very slow-growing tumor, so we don't have to rush her into emergency surgery tonight. They will schedule an appointment with you to talk all about it, hopefully tomorrow."

*Surgery?* Wasn't that a fancy word for cutting someone open and fixing stuff inside them? Were they going to open up my head? I didn't like that idea very much.

Today went from guacamole to needing brain surgery.

Boo.

Triple boo.

Super-ultra-quadrillion boo.

The doctor turned to me. "Do you understand, Maddie?"

I nodded, though it was kind of a lie. I really didn't understand.

My dad walked over and hugged me. My mom grabbed a tissue and quickly wiped her eyes.

"Do you have any questions for me?" the doctor asked.

I didn't want to talk to the doctor. I wanted to talk to my mom and dad. I shook my head.

The doctor kept talking. "After it's all done, you'll get to go on these really cool beds where you can push buttons and move your head up or down and your feet up or down. You can move it into all sorts of positions so you can be really comfortable."

That sounded pretty cool. My bed at home didn't have any buttons.

The doctor smiled. "And I heard that the nurses will let you order whatever you want from the menu to eat. So you could get a brownie or spaghetti or French fries."

I liked brownies and French fries, but I didn't want to try to figure out what was going on anymore. I looked away, and the doctor went back to talking to my parents.

"Hey, Maddie," Max whispered. Under his red hair and blue eyes, he was wearing a mustache made out of orange Play-Doh. The room didn't feel like it was a place for laughing, but I did. He looked so hilarious. And honestly, it felt good to laugh. Really good. The rest of the room was so stuffy and serious. "I made it for you," he said. He peeled the Play-Doh mustache off his upper lip and handed it to me.

"Thanks," I said and took the glob of clay. I loved it. It was a little gross and a lot cute.

I loved all kinds of different mustaches, but right then, that one was my all-time favorite. Not just anything could make me laugh when I found out I needed surgery on my brain.

# CHAPTER 11

# Ice Cream for Breakfast

"Eggs taste gross," Emery said.

"Why can't we have cereal?" Ethan asked.

"Because I made eggs," Mom said.

"If you loved us, you'd make us pancakes," Emery said.

"Yeah, I vote for pancakes," Ethan agreed. The twins had a way of trying to sound like the majority of the family.

"Nobody said we'd be voting this morning," Mom said. She spotted me coming in. "Maddie, aren't you tired?" Her voice was overly cheery, like when she was either exhausted or grumpy. "Do you want to go back to bed?" We had been at the hospital until after dinnertime, and by the time we got some food and drove all the way back home, it was really late. Then it took me a while to fall asleep. That didn't usually happen, but yesterday wasn't a usual day. I had a real monster to think about. Not just a made-up Dragoporkisaur but a haunting terror. Something horrifying and unknown waiting in the darkness to get me.

I shook my head. No one had woken me up to get ready for school. It would be time to leave in fifteen minutes, and I wasn't ready at all. I hadn't slept well. I didn't want to go to school. And I didn't want to go back to bed either.

"Can *I* go back to sleep?" Ethan asked, fake yawning and scratching his crazy-messy hair.

"Yeah, me too," Emery said.

"No," Mom said. She set the frying pan on a cold burner.

I sat down at the kitchen table next to Max.

"Maddie, are you gonna die?" Max asked. He asked it like he was asking for pancakes. There wasn't anything different about his voice—no tears, no emotion, just curiosity.

*Die?* I hadn't thought about that.

That felt heavy. Like a thousand pounds on my heart.

"She's not going to die," Mom said, facing us. "I told you that she is going to have surgery so they can take out her tumor."

"But you said this was serious and we had to pray for her every day," Ethan said.

"That's true," Mom said. "But she's going to be fine."

"I drew this for you," Emery said and handed me a card. It showed a crayon version of me with a big head and yellow hair.

Above it were the words *I love you, Maddie*. That made me feel all gushy inside. Maybe the twins weren't completely evil after all. I opened up the card.

*"I hope you don't die, but if you do, can I have your money and your candy?"*

Okay. Maybe still a little evil. That was more like what I was expecting.

"And I drew this one," Ethan said.

As he handed me a card that said "Get well" on the front, my mom explained, "Grandma and Grandpa watched them yesterday while we were at the hospital. They made you cards."

"Thanks," I said.

"Grandma and Grandpa wanted me to hug you super-tight," Mom said as she hugged me, "and tell you that they are praying for you."

It seemed like everyone was praying for me. I knew Grandma and Grandpa prayed for me all the time. They prayed I would grow up nice and healthy and smart and awesome, but this felt different. Were they praying that I wouldn't die?

I felt cold.

My mom started to explain to the boys everything the doctor had said. I felt bad, like I'd gotten a really bad grade, except it wasn't a grade for a term. It was a grade for life.

"Hey, girl," Dad said, walking into the kitchen. He sometimes got to work in his office at home. He walked over and gave me a big hug. He didn't let go right away. "I'm sorry about this," he whispered. "Everything is going to be just fine." I liked hearing it, but it meant that there was a chance that everything might not be fine.

"Maybe I *will* go back to bed," I said.

"I wish I could do that," Dad said.

"You can if you want to," Mom said, then quickly turned to everyone else. "I'm talking to Maddie. Not dad or the twins or Max." All of the boys moaned. My dad's was fake, but the twins did it for real. Apparently if you have a tumor you get to do all sorts of things. "Give me just a minute, and I'll come to your room and talk to you," Mom said to me.

I nodded.

"And I'll come right now," Dad said.

He followed me out of the kitchen, down the hall, and into my room. I flopped onto my comforter. It was really fluffy and had a whole bunch of mustaches printed on it. Funny— but I wasn't laughing. I didn't feel like it. Dad lifted the mustache blanket up, and I snuggled into the fluffiness and closed my eyes. I was hoping to fall asleep superfast before Dad could talk or Mom came in.

It didn't work.

"Try not to worry too much," Dad said and rubbed my back. Again, I liked it, but it meant there was a reason to be afraid. It was like telling me not to worry about a monster.

I heard my door open and felt Mom sit down on my bed next to Dad.

"When you wake up, you can have ice cream for breakfast," Mom said. I pulled the covers off my face and smiled. That sounded great. I had never had ice cream for breakfast in my whole life. Mom was doing a lot better job of cheering me up than Dad.

Mom ran her fingers through my hair. "Are you okay?"

I nodded, but of course I wasn't. I wished I could go back to yesterday when I was a little slow and trippy and my hand didn't work but my brain was fine.

"Don't worry," she said and kissed my forehead. When I was little, I thought Mom's kisses could cure anything. I wished she could kiss away my tumor.

"Is there anything you want to say? To ask about?" Dad asked.

I shook my head. I didn't want to talk; I wanted to pull the covers back over my head.

"Then we'll let you sleep," Mom said.

"Wait a second," Dad said. "I have an idea." Uh-oh. Dad having an idea wasn't always a good thing. "The surgery is scheduled for a little over two weeks from now. I think we should go on a vacation before that."

"Really?" I asked. Dad just pulled ahead big-time.

"I'm not sure we have the money," Mom said.

"I'll find it," Dad said. That was weird. My dad was usually the one who worried about money, and my mom was the one wanting to go on vacation. "We should do something really fun all together before we have to worry about this medical stuff." He smiled at me. "Where would you want to go for a few days?"

I didn't even have to think about it. I knew. "Disneyland," I said. I had gone there when I was in the first grade, but I couldn't really remember it. Cassie said she went there every year.

"Done," Dad said. He was totally winning.

"But what about your book?" Mom asked. Dad had a ton of stuff to get ready before his book release and tour.

"I'll play during the day and get my work done at night," he said. I liked his smile, but it already looked tired.

"Okay," Mom said. She turned back to me. "Dream about that. But first, I wanted to ask if you're okay if I talk to your teacher and let her know what's going on."

I didn't know what to say. That would change things. Mrs. Baer was super nice, but I didn't know if things would be different once she knew I had something weird in my head. And would the class find out? Would they think I was some sort of freak? Maybe because of my weird arm, some of them had been thinking it for a long time.

"She's going to have to find out sooner or later," Dad said.

"Okay, but not yet," I said. I didn't want everyone else to know. Especially not Cassie.

Mom agreed, and I pulled the covers over my head and tried to think about Disneyland.

# CHAPTER 12

# Did You Ask Him?

When the bell rang for recess, Cassie walked with me, and only me, down the hall. She'd never done that before. Maybe we were best buds now. That was good. With everything I found out yesterday, I needed a best bud. She had her blonde hair in curls today and wore a shirt with sleeves that looked like a lacy tablecloth. The white kind with fancy twists and flower-shaped spaces you can see the table through. Super cute. As always.

My mom had dropped me off late after my ice cream for breakfast. I couldn't really sleep, and we decided that it was best for now if we tried to live as normal as possible until Disneyland and then the surgery. I was going to miss quite a bit of school. I tried to think more about the vacation part than the surgery part. My mom walked me all the way to my classroom, but then waited outside. I didn't want her to give anyone the hint that anything was wrong.

"I'm going to Disneyla—" I started. I knew Cassie would want to hear it. She loves to tell us all about the trips her family takes every year.

"Did you ask him yet?" Cassie interrupted me.

Ask who what? My mind had to think for a second. Ask someone about Disneyland? No. Ask the doctor when I was going to have surgery on my brain? Ask if I was going to die? Did she know? How would she know?

"Did you ask Devin?" Cassie whispered, obviously seeing my confusion.

Oh, yeah. My secret mission. "Not yet," I said.

"Why not?" Cassie asked. She was giving me her "I'm the boss, and I'm disappointed in you" face. Maybe we weren't best buds yet. "You've had lots of time." She sounded like a mom getting after her kid who hadn't cleaned their room. Maybe Cassie's mom talked like that.

"Um. Because I was in the hospital all day yesterday and found out that I have some giant tumor in my head messing up my brain and my eyes and the left side of my body like a monster watching and waiting to gobble me up, and I might die." That was the best excuse in the universe.

But I didn't say it.

I couldn't.

"Sorry," I said, opening the door to go outside. Cassie walked out first. I followed. "I've been really busy. But I did find out that I'm going to Disneyland."

"Really? Oh."

Not quite the reaction I was looking for.

"Well," she said and gave out one of her little huffs, "ask Devin soon because I want you to hang out with me, but you can't until you ask him." Then she gave me a big painted smile.

"Okay," I said. I didn't know what else to say.

Cassie continued toward the walking path, the other girls following. I lagged behind. At least she wanted to hang out with me. I guess that was something on my terrible day-after-I-found-out-I-had-a-tumor day. But with each step, what Cassie had said felt less and less nice. Why couldn't she let me hang out with her now? Why did I have to ask Devin first? She had asked me to do it as a favor, but it didn't feel like that anymore. It was almost like she really was some queen and had banished me from the kingdom until I went on a quest for her.

Yasmin had been following Cassie, but paused. "Aren't you coming?"

"I've got to do something," I said. "I'll catch up."

"Does it have to do with a huge pig-dragon monster?" she asked, a smile on her face.

"Maybe," I said with a grin and a wink. I wanted to tell her about my secret mission. I wanted her to help me, but Cassie probably wouldn't have liked that. I wanted to tell Yasmin about my tumor even more. Maybe she would have something to say, something that would help. Maybe she would hug me and tell me it would all be okay.

Or maybe she would think I was a freak.

I didn't say anything.

"Okay, hurry and meet us on the track," she said and ran to catch up with Cassie.

I didn't want to do any of it. I wanted to collapse and cry. But I didn't have anywhere to go. My bed was back home, and I didn't have a mustache blanket to pull over my head. I could call my mom and she would pick me up. But then what would I do? Worry and cry? I knew I couldn't sleep. Maybe I could think about Disneyland. No. I knew even that would fade and I would end up depressed.

It wasn't my favorite option, but I decided to accomplish my secret mission. At least I would be thinking about something other than my tumor.

It would be easiest to talk to Devin when I was walking home after school, but I didn't want to wait that long. My life had been hard enough lately without spending recess alone. I wanted to ask him soon and get back to hanging out with Cassie and Yasmin and the others.

I knew just where to find Devin: the basketball court. He loved basketball. He always had. He wore an LA Clippers jersey at least once a week. I thought Clippers was a weird name for a basketball team. Were they like haircutters, or did they take care of the lawn? Anyway, Devin even played on some super-sweet team that went places on the weekends to compete.

Okay. Go to the basketball court. But I had to get there before they started playing, or I couldn't ask him until . . .

Too late.

The boys had already picked teams and started the game. And I wasn't about to go over there and stop them all to ask Devin who he liked in front of everyone. Then my mission wouldn't be secret at all. Plus, all the boys would probably think that I liked Devin. Which of course I didn't. I mean, sure, he's cute and nice and can be funny, but it wasn't like when he looked at me his face went all in slow motion and my heart start thumping really fast like in the movies. And I definitely didn't want everyone else thinking it was.

Devin dribbled the ball down the court, faked one way, then drove the other toward the basket. When a few guys on the other team tried to defend him, he passed to Ryan, who was wide open for the easy shot.

Pretty good.

But now I had to wait until the end of recess and try to "happen" to walk next to him as we went back to class. And I had no one to hang out with.

"Hey, Maddie," someone said.

Who was talking to me?

# CHAPTER 13

# Crossing the Sahara

I turned to see Lexi looking at me. She was wearing a cute dark blue shirt with a matching bow in her hair.

"Hey, Lexi," I said, probably a little too loudly. I was pretty excited not to be alone.

"Cassie wouldn't let me hang out with her. You neither?"

I didn't want to admit it because I was doing a favor for Cassie. This wasn't a normal situation. It wasn't like I didn't get chosen. Okay. Maybe that wasn't entirely right, but it felt different than not getting picked.

"Not today," I said.

"Well," Lexi said, "is it okay if we hang out?" Normally Cassie wouldn't like that, but I needed someone right now.

"Sure," I said. "What do you want to do?" I had to do something to pass the time before the end of recess when I could meet up with Devin.

"I dunno. The monkey bars?" she asked.

I almost agreed, but my arm. I used to be good at the monkey bars, but I'd noticed a while ago that I wasn't anymore. That was actually my first clue that my arm was a little weird. I had avoided them ever since. "How about we pretend we're trying to cross the Sahara to rescue a kidnapped millionaire before we die of thirst," I said.

"What?" Lexi said.

Maybe I shouldn't have said whatever crazy thing came into my mind. "We just walk around and talk and stuff." I shrugged. "Oh, and we can pretend we're thirsty if we want."

Lexi nodded and smiled. I imagined that if I was in Lexi's shoes, I would love to have someone to be with. New school. Not many friends.

"So what's up with you?" Lexi asked.

An MRI.

A huge tumor.

I might die.

Of course I didn't tell her.

"Other than crossing the Sahara and my parched throat? I'm going to Disneyland soon," I said. I did feel comfortable saying that.

"Really?" Lexi asked. I guess after the whole desert thing,

it was tough to know if I was telling the truth. When I confirmed it was for real, Lexi brightened up. "I've never been, but I hear it's really fun." That was more of what I hoped Cassie would have said.

"Yeah. I hope it is." And I really did. I hoped it was the best vacation ever. One so good that I'd forget all about my surgery. "And I'm pretty excited about the Shakespeare plays. I really want to know what part I have."

"Me too," Lexi said. "I want to be Viola in *Twelfth Night*."

"Oh, she would be great," I said. "She gets in an awesome mess." While she's pretending to be a boy, Viola meets this guy and really likes him. The problem? He thinks she's just one of the boys. Then the guy sends her with love letters to a different girl. And that girl, thinking Viola is a boy, falls in love with her. A crazy mess. Lexi had good taste.

"How about you?" she asked.

I told her about Hamlet or Katherine. I left out the Juliet part.

"This morning Mrs. Baer said she would announce our parts before the end of the day," Lexi said.

Awesome. I could really use some good news after yesterday. "Good," I said. "And what have you been up to?" I glanced over at the boys playing basketball. Devin was guarding Coby. I wasn't lucky enough for him to leave to get a drink or want to sit out for a minute.

"I got to see my dad last night."

"Your dad?"

"Yeah, it's been a while. I usually go over there every other weekend, but he's been out of town."

Her parents must be divorced. I didn't know that. I imagined that might be tough, not being with both your parents all the time. I didn't want to go a week without seeing my dad.

"So what did you do?"

"We got some sweet-pork burritos and smoothies. I doubt it's as cool as Disneyland, but I love smoothies."

At least she got to have some fun with her dad.

"Yay for smoothies. But pork?" I thought of Dragoporkisaur. "Nope to meat. Potatoes are the best." I looked at the court again. Devin was running beneath the basket with his hand up, calling for the ball.

"Potatoes are definitely not the best."

"What about sweet-potato fries?" I asked.

"Those aren't real potatoes, but they are pretty good."

"Yes, they are—and *yes, they are.* Especially since we're both starving in the desert."

Lexi laughed again.

We walked for a while, and I really liked it. I didn't have to force anything to say, stuff just came out. And Lexi liked my crazy thoughts, listened, asked stuff back, and played along. I thought Yasmin would like her, too. I didn't see why Cassie wouldn't let her hang out with us.

We were coming up on the basketball court so I checked to see if Devin was still playing. Yep.

Lexi smirked at me. "Why are you looking over at the boys on the basketball court so much?" she asked.

She thought I had a crush. I'm sure I turned red. "What? Those aren't boys. They're just a mirage." Good one. My slightly damaged brain thinks fast sometimes.

"Well, then, why do you keep looking back at that mirage?" Lexi said. "Do you like one of those mirages better than the others?"

"No. I have to find out who one of them likes," I said. "For a friend," I added.

"Really? So they aren't just mirages?" Lexi's eyebrow went up. "Which friend?"

I thought for a second. "The bandit empress of the dunes," I said.

Lexi nodded. "And you aren't going to tell me who that is, are you?"

I shook my head, though I wondered if she guessed it was Cassie.

"So it's kind of like *Twelfth Night*," Lexi said. "You're the messenger trying to help two people get together."

"Yeah. Kind of," I said. "Except I'm not pretending to be a boy."

"But maybe whoever you are asking will fall in love with you instead of whoever you are asking for," Lexi said.

"No way." But I'm pretty sure I blushed.

"Which boy do you have to ask?" Lexi asked.

"You mean which mirage? The one that looks like Devin," I said.

This time Lexi reddened. We took a few more steps together, but Lexi was fidgety.

"Do you want me to tell you what I find out?" I asked.

She smiled big and nodded. I was pretty sure she didn't want the boy to fall in love with the messenger anymore.

"Okay," I said. "But I might need some help."

"What do you mean?" Lexi asked.

"Well, all the boys are always together," I said. "If you could distract some of them, then I could talk to Devin—or the mirage that looks like him."

"I can try," she said. "But what would I do?"

"I don't know." Maybe she could lead them all into a trap, like quicksand. Or tranquilize them with blow darts. No. That wouldn't work on mirages. Or she could . . . "Wait." I actually had an idea. "Ask them who won and who scored the most and stuff like that. Boys like to talk about stuff that makes them seem cooler. Trust me. I have brothers."

"But I'm kind of shy," Lexi said.

I shrugged. "Me too," I said. "But I think we can do this."

Lexi thought for a second and then nodded.

The bell rang.

Recess was over. Time for action.

# CHAPTER 14

# Asking

"That was awesome," Cesar said. "I was on fire."

"What?" Coby asked. "Were you playing a different game, because that never happened."

"Um," Cesar said, "you must have hit your head while trying to defend me, because it definitely happened."

"I think you came closer to hitting my head than the basket," Coby said.

I moved behind them on the way back to the school. I had to talk to Devin before we got to class, but I couldn't do it in front of all of his friends. I passed a few girls playing four square and walked behind the boys.

Now it was up to Lexi.

I waited, hoping.

Hoping.

They came closer to the door. I looked for Lexi, but I couldn't see her in the crowd of kids coming back in from recess. What would I do if she backed out?

"Hey, guys," Lexi said from the other side of Cesar. "How did basketball go?"

Wow. She had told me she was shy, but she jumped right in. Impressive.

"Awesome," Cesar said. "I was like an all-star, driving and swishing everything I shot. I think I got my personal record for points this recess."

"He only hit one basket," Coby said. "And apparently that's his record."

Cesar swatted him.

The distraction was definitely working. The other friends soon joined in. Few things are as tempting to a boy as showing off in front of a girl. Devin stepped toward them. I had to act fast.

I rushed out from behind the group. I was only a few steps away.

And then it happened. My leg froze midstep, sending me tumbling to the ground, bumbling and crying out as I fell.

Not in the plan.

Maybe they didn't notice. Maybe they were so distracted by Lexi that they would walk past. I looked up, knowing I probably had dirt and blacktop rocks in my hair and across my face. Coby and Cesar erupted in laughter.

They definitely noticed.

Devin jogged over to me. "You okay?" he asked, offering me his hand. Boy hands felt weird. His was warm and sweaty. He helped me up easily, maybe even pulling too hard to show how strong he was. I thought about *Twelfth Night*. That would be awkward—Devin liking me. Well, not completely awkward, but not likely with blacktop rocks on my face. I brushed my cheeks just in case the little rocks were there.

Cesar and Coby bobbed up and down behind Devin, unable to control themselves.

"It's not funny, you two," Devin said.

Cesar nodded but let out a snort. And that made Coby snort in return. Double snort. I almost broke out in a laugh at that.

"So who won?" Lexi asked, trying to save me. The two turned back to her quicker than a crossover dribble. Thank you, Lexi.

"Sorry," I apologized to Devin. "I'm pretty clumsy sometimes."

Yep, ever since I went up for a backflip dunk and hit both my left arm and leg against the rim while I was rotating, they hadn't worked so well. Of course, I still made the dunk.

"Me too," Devin said. I couldn't picture that. He was a good athlete. Every move seemed smooth and calculated. He looked over at Lexi, probably making sure his friends weren't still laughing at me.

"I have to ask you a question," I blurted out, trying to get it over with. "Cas . . ." I stopped myself. "Somebody wants me to ask . . ." I tried to clear my throat quietly. I felt sheepish even asking, but I had to do it. Otherwise I couldn't hang out with Cassie. "Who do you like?"

Devin blushed, his eyes moving to the side.

I didn't expect that, though I'm not sure why. He looked back at me and then over his shoulder at Lexi. His cheeks deepened a darker shade of red.

"Nobod . . . I don't . . . I'm not answering that," he said.

But I was pretty sure he already had. This was not like *Twelfth Night*. Devin wasn't interested in the messenger. It was pretty clear he liked Lexi.

It bothered me a little. Silly, I know, but whenever I heard that a boy liked another girl I felt a little jealous. Like I was less than she was.

"What about . . . Cassie?" I asked, trying to sound like I was picking out a random name. I had to be sure.

"No," he said, shaking his head. "I mean. She's pretty and stuff, but no."

I nodded.

Part of me was thrilled for Lexi, but the other part didn't want to tell Cassie. This was not what she wanted to hear.

# CHAPTER 15

# Casting

Cassie waved me over to the corner of the room. Everyone was still coming back in from recess, and class hadn't gotten started yet. Lexi saw that I had talked to Devin, but Cesar and Coby were still telling her about the basketball game.

"Did you ask him?" Cassie asked me.

I nodded.

"And?" She was practically bouncing.

What was I going to say? "He wouldn't tell me," I said. That was technically true.

"What?" she asked, her expression instantly falling. What had she expected? For him to dramatically confess his love for her? Um, he was a sixth-grade boy. Cassie moved in closer, still talking quietly. "But he doesn't like Lexi, does he?"

"What?" I asked. Had she been watching? Had she seen him look at Lexi and blush?

"Oh," she said, "I heard Cesar talking to Coby one day. I don't know for sure if they were talking about Devin or not, but they mentioned that someone liked Lexi."

"I'm not sure," I said and shrugged. Of course I was 97½% sure that Devin did like Lexi.

Cassie looked away and back again. She exhaled long and hard, like she was trying to calm down and keep in either tears or screams. Maybe both. She smiled big and blinked a few times. I suspected she hadn't had to deal with disappointment much.

"So can we hang out at lunch?" I asked. I had done everything she asked.

Cassie looked at me for a second, and her fake smile left. "Why were you hanging out with Lexi?" Apparently she had seen us walking around at recess.

What should I say? I knew Cassie didn't like Lexi, but Lexi had just been really helpful. And she was fun to be around. I shrugged. "She asked, and I didn't want her to be lonely." Maybe that wasn't the entire truth. She kept me from being lonely, too.

Cassie looked at me strangely. Maybe it was the same way

she looked at Lexi. Maybe she was starting not to like me, either. "I think you should stop it," she said.

"To your seats, please," Mrs. Baer said.

Cassie's hands rested on her hips for a moment before she spun and went to her desk. I still couldn't tell if she was mad at the situation, or at me, or both. I probably wouldn't know until recess.

I wanted to talk to Lexi, but Mrs. Baer got us started on state capitals. My favorite was Tallahassee. Weird word. Really fun to say.

Finally, when we'd both finished our assignments, I whispered over to her. "You were an awesome distraction."

"Thanks," Lexi whispered back. "Sorry you tripped."

"That's okay," I said.

"What did you find out about you-know-who?" She was blushing already.

"He didn't say it," I said, "but I think he likes someone in our class."

Lexi pointed toward Cassie and raised her eyebrows.

I shook my head. "I think it might be a girl with brown hair who is great at being a distraction."

I didn't think a person's face could turn that red.

"Now, before we go to lunch," Mrs. Baer said. "I have some news you've been waiting for." Everyone moved up in their seats, murmuring about parts to the play. My heart beat superfast. "But before any official announcements, I need to tell you a few things." Mrs. Baer gave the speech everyone knew was coming. It was about how we were all talented and how lots of us could have done all of the leads, but they had to pick someone. It was kind of useless. Not because it wasn't true or nice. It was. It was just useless because when someone doesn't get a good part, they feel bad. And that happens whether or not your teacher gives a speech.

"The fairy queen will be played by Hannah Williams," Mrs. Baer said. "And the fairy king by Coby Ahmed."

A few of the guys pushed Coby. He looked a little embarrassed. Hannah was beaming.

"Sailor, Yasmin, and Jen will be fairies. And Ford will be Bottom."

Everyone laughed at that. Bottom was a character's name in *A Midsummer Night's Dream*. And if that wasn't funny enough, he was the guy who got his head changed to a donkey head. So awesome.

Mrs. Baer continued to announce part after part for what seemed like forever. I didn't get Hamlet. No poison-tipped sword fighting for me.

When Lexi got Viola in *Twelfth Night*, I gave her a high five. As soon as I had, I hoped Cassie hadn't seen.

"And Cassie will be playing Juliet," Mrs. Baer said.

That was to be expected. She was the prettiest and a really good actress.

Except for that wasn't what Mrs. Baer said. I had expected

it so much that it took me a moment to realize that Mrs. Baer had said something different.

"And Cassie," she had said, "will be playing Bianca."

Not Juliet.

Cassie's mouth spread into a forced smile. She looked like a perfect plastic doll. She looked around the room as if trying to find out who'd gotten the part that was destined for her. My stomach did all sorts of backflips while Mrs. Baer finished the *Taming of the Shrew* cast. I was a little disappointed I hadn't gotten Katherine.

Only one play left.

"Devin will be playing Romeo," Mrs. Baer said. There was more teasing and pushing for this announcement than any other. Devin blushed bright red. I didn't think any of the boys wanted that part. At least they would never admit it.

Cassie's smile became a little more fake.

"And Juliet will be played by . . ." Mrs. Baer paused.

My little heart was banging like a drum, but the drummer had eaten way too much sugar, plus drank a few sodas, and downed some Pixy Stix. Seriously, it was going crazy.

"Maddie Bridger," Mrs. Baer said.

Yes!

Wait. I could feel Cassie glaring at me.

Oh, no.

# CHAPTER 16

# Mix-Up

"Maddie," Cassie said. When we lined up for lunch, she purposefully stood right next to me. And she wasn't smiling. "How did you get Juliet? I thought you were going to be Juliet's nurse."

I shrugged. "That was what *you* wanted. Not what *I* wanted."

Nope. You guessed it. I didn't really say that. Part of me wished I could be that honest with Cassie, but I just couldn't. I mean, she was Cassie. But I did shrug.

"Then how did you get it?"

I shrugged again. Though I had put it down on my paper and I had auditioned for it, I really had no idea how I got the part. Who would pick me over Cassie? I wasn't as tall or as pretty, and my arm and leg were weird.

"There must be some sort of mix-up," Cassie said. "Come on." She grabbed my arm, we stepped out of line, and marched up to Mrs. Baer, who was leading the class.

"Mrs. Baer," Cassie said. Her painted smile was definitely back. "I think there might have been some sort of mistake." Her tone was perfect. Cassie had a way of talking to adults that made her sound like the sweetest thing. It's not that she wasn't sweet, just not as sweet as she sounded. "I really wanted to play Juliet, and Maddie didn't even request that part."

Mrs. Baer looked surprised and then turned toward me. Oh, no. Here was when she would say something like, "Yes, she did. It was her first choice." And all of the kids walking behind Mrs. Baer in the lunch line would hear us. And Cassie would hate me more. And then I would never get to hang out with her again.

Which, of course, might not matter since I had a tumor in my head and might not live much longer anyway.

I braced myself for the worst.

But Mrs. Baer turned back toward Cassie. "You would have made a marvelous Juliet, but we chose to give the part to Maddie. She'll do a great job too."

"But I really want it, and I didn't even put down Bianca and—" Cassie started.

"No," Mrs. Baer cut her off. "There is no use complaining.

We have made our decision. But you will make a wonderful Bianca. Now fall back into your place in line."

Cassie looked like she was going to say something again.

We were just entering the cafeteria, and Mrs. Baer waited by the door as the class filed past her. "Wait with me, Maddie. I want to ask you something."

Cassie didn't look very pleased, but there wasn't much she could do. I felt like I was in trouble as everyone else in my class walked by. Cassie merged back in line, but I could tell by the rhythm of her walk that she wasn't happy.

Mrs. Baer led me away from the cafeteria.

I braced myself. Was she going to talk about the part? Or worse, had she somehow heard about my tumor? Was she going to ask me about it? Was she going to tell everyone?

"Maddie, you did request Juliet," Mrs. Baer said. "Why did you tell Cassie something else?"

"I . . ." I started. I didn't know how to explain it, but there was something about Mrs. Baer that made it easier to talk to her. "I guess because I knew she really wanted it, and I didn't want her mad at me."

Mrs. Baer looked at me, and I was pretty sure she could read my thoughts. Some teachers have that power. "You know you don't have to please everyone."

I blinked.

"It's okay to just be you. If Cassie doesn't like it, that's fine."

I nodded. Did Mrs. Baer actually think that I would do a

better job playing Juliet? Or was she trying to teach me to be myself even if Cassie didn't like it? Or was it both? I wanted to ask her why she chose me, but all I said was "Thanks."

Mrs. Baer walked me to the end of our class line. I didn't bother trying to move up by Cassie. She was almost to the food anyway. As I got my tray and utensils, I wasn't really sure I even cared about lunch anymore. Partly because I was thinking about how much Cassie was upset, and partly because of my tumor, and partly because they weren't serving any potatoes.

I really could have used some potatoes.

As I walked out of the line with my food, looking for a place to sit, I saw Cassie with Sailor and Hannah and Yasmin and the rest of the girls, the group I'd tried to hang out with all year. It was the group I'd just risked a lot for to find out who Devin liked. A group I'd wished would give me a break from worrying about a tumor in my head. And that group was looking right at me. But Cassie was pointing. No one waved for me to come join them.

Lexi did from a different table, but Cassie didn't want me to hang out with her either.

I sat down by myself, still remembering Mrs. Baer's words. It was okay to just be me. Just be me. I really wanted to believe it, but it was hard sitting alone at a lunch table with my old friends pointing at me.

# CHAPTER 17

# Meeting Romeo

Devin looked at me, then back down at his script. He wiped his palms against his pants and started. "But, soft! what light through yonder window breaks? It is the east, and Juliet is the sun."

I know. It's super mushy stuff. Apparently he was in love with me. Not Devin, but Romeo. It felt weird, but I didn't hate it. We were just doing a read-through of our script. We only had four weeks to get ready for our performances, but Mrs. Baer said we would practice every day. She wanted us to try to be memorized in a week. That's superfast, but our scenes were only a few minutes long. Good thing I have a genius brain.

"It is my lady, O, it is my love! O, that she knew she were!"

He said it all with his face almost buried in his folder. He sounded more like a robot than an actor. I wanted to say that he didn't have to worry, that I knew he didn't really like me, that we were only pretending. He probably would have been crazy red if Lexi had gotten Juliet's part.

"See, how she leans her cheek upon her hand," Devin said, still not looking up.

Oh, sweet-potato fries! Apparently I was supposed to be leaning my cheek against my hand. I hadn't noticed at all. That would be really funny if he said that in the play but when everyone looked at me I was in the totally wrong position. I rested my head on my right hand. My left hand was balled in a fist again and starting to tuck back. Probably not the best Juliet position.

"O, that I were a glove upon that hand, that I might touch that cheek!"

Really, Shakespeare? Romeo wanted to be a glove? Super-de-duper mush-a-rrific. I mean I liked love stories, but that was a bit much.

But I also didn't totally hate it.

Oh. It was my line. I wasn't paying attention. I looked down at my script, found my place, and quickly called out. "Ay me!"

Yep. That was my first line. Shakespeare is famous for making up the best plays in the world, and my first line in my scene was "Ay me!" That would never jump-start my career as a famous actress.

Devin talked more, calling me a "bright angel" and "a winged messenger of heaven." I was pretty sure he was wishing he was sword fighting right now. Or maybe even wishing his head had been changed to a donkey head.

Oh, no, my turn again. "O Romeo, Romeo! wherefore art thou Romeo?" I pretended I was on some high balcony looking over a courtyard.

"Uh, I'm right here," Devin said. I guess he thought he could relax and joke around now that it was my line. Well, it worked. We both laughed.

"I was trying to act, but you just blew it," I said.

"Yeah," he said, his lips curling up for a change.

Was I the only one listening when Mrs. Baer explained that *wherefore* meant *why*? At least he was having fun.

There was a moment of silence as we both looked for our spots in the script. "This is a little awkward, huh?" I said.

"Yeah," he agreed.

"Maybe we should do it again," I said, "but wearing mustaches." I tried to make the mustaches sound as exciting as I could. I pulled two of them from my pocket.

Devin looked at them for a second, then a smile slowly crept over his face. "I get the fuzzy black one."

"What?" I said. "So selfish. But I guess that's okay."

We both put them on and tried the scene again. This time,

we about died laughing at every other line. I caught Cassie glaring at us a few times from the other side of the room, but I tried to ignore her. When a guy in a big bushy black mustache was calling me "a winged messenger of heaven," I was going to pay attention. You don't get a lot of those opportunities in life.

Shakespeare should always be done with mustaches.

We made it through our first scene before the last bell rang. We still had one more to go.

"That was fun," Devin said and took off his mustache.

"Yeah, it was," I said, taking mine off too. When I took his mustache from him, our hands touched a little, but I pretended not to notice. Maybe being Juliet would be a great thing. Maybe Mrs. Baer would actually let us perform in mustaches. Well, probably not me. But even if Devin could, that might make it more fun. And maybe it would be the best scene of all of them. Maybe the crowd would laugh and cry and clap loud and long at the end, standing on their feet in a teary ovation.

It was only after I grabbed my backpack that I remembered about my tumor. The monster waiting for me. I could almost picture its eyes like glowing fires watching patiently, waiting for the perfect time to attack.

It sure had been nice to forget.

# CHAPTER 18

# The List I
# Super-Ultra-Mega Hated

*Thank you for hanging out with me today. I had a lot of fun. And you have a great imagination.*

Lexi

*P.S. You're going to make a great Juliet!*

I found the little card in my backpack when I unloaded it after school. I took it with me in the car. And I read it one last time before the neurosurgeon walked into the room. The neurosurgeon—that's a fancy word for a brain doctor—looked down at me. Her name was Dr. Montoya. She had short hair, golden-brown skin, and wore a white lab coat. Apparently those are super fashionable at hospitals and in doctor's offices. She took a deep breath.

"Maddie only has three days to live. There's nothing we can do."

Three days.

My heart plummeted. Three days? As the reality set in, my heart sunk even further. I was only going to have a couple of days to squeeze in everything I ever wanted to do? Could we still go to Disneyland? Maybe I could fit in a little skydiving. Maybe my first film role? Oh, and taking over a small country, crowning myself queen, making every day a holiday in which all the people would have to cook me my favorite meals of potatoes.

Okay, the neurosurgeon didn't say that. Thank heavens. I had been day-nightmaring she would. I had also been hoping that she wouldn't say, "This tumor is actually a living creature and is feeding on Maddie's brain. In a while, it will take over her body and use it to take over the world, make her queen, and make every day a holiday in which all the people would have to cook her meals of potatoes." That would be a bummer because my body would be taken over and I wouldn't get to enjoy any of the potatoes.

But I did talk to Dr. Montoya. We were at my appointment to talk about my surgery. She was really calm, and older than my mom but younger than my grandma.

"So," Dr. Montoya said, "from the images we can see, we believe that the tumor is actually on Maddie's pituitary gland."

Pitui-what?

"It's the part of the body that regulates growth, maturation, blood pressure, and hormones. And the tumor is pressing up against her brain and optic nerves. To get as much of it out as we can, we'd like to do what's called a transsphenoidal approach."

*Pituitary? Transsphenoidal?* Was she making these words up?

"Which basically means we will use little tubes and go up through Maddie's nose until we reach just under the brain." She was mostly talking to my mom and dad.

Whoa. Do you remember in first grade how you used to make jokes that you should be careful about picking your nose because you could scratch your brain? Well, apparently if your finger was long enough, it just might work. But I didn't like the idea of anything scratching my brain.

Dr. Montoya explained that some of the tubes had tiny cameras so the doctors could see what they were doing, which I thought sounded pretty awesome. Some of the other tubes had tools on them to chop up the tumor, and some had sucky things to suck it out. It was the most disgusting and amazing explanation ever. Of course, it would have been a whole lot cooler if all those tubes were going into someone else's head.

My nose was too small, though, so they were going to cut

a little hole under my top lip but above my gums and shove all of those tubes into my brain. I couldn't stop running my tongue over that area of my mouth after she told me.

Ready for the weirdest part?

Then they were going to cut my stomach and take some fat tissue out to plug up the hole they made. It was supposed to keep my brain fluid from leaking out.

Tummy fat shoved through my mouth? Weird. And kind of awesome.

But mostly weird.

I really hoped that I wouldn't accidentally wake up while they were doing any of those things.

"How many times have you done this surgery?" my dad asked.

I would have never thought about that question, but now that my dad asked it, I thought it was a really good one. I didn't want someone who had never done this before messing around with my brain.

"Brain surgeries? Over a thousand times. Most of which were transsphenoidal," Dr. Montoya said.

Seriously? This lady had messed with people's heads over a thousand times? I hoped all of them ended really well.

"And are you the best doctor to do it?" my dad asked. Wow. Bold. He was in total business mode. I'd seen him get this way about his books. It was a "Don't mess with me, and let's get this done right" sort of mode.

"She is one of the best in the world," the doctor's assistant said. "If it were my son or daughter, I would have Dr. Montoya do the surgery."

The doctor stood there awkwardly, accepting the compliment. "But if you would like," the doctor said, "you could look into UCLA or the Mayo Clinic. They both have some very strong neurosurgeons dealing with this kind of tumor."

My dad nodded. You could bet your hash browns he would look into them.

"Will her arm and leg go back to normal after the surgery?" Mom asked.

"We don't know," Dr. Montoya said. "We would expect them to regain at least some of their movement, but it depends on how much the tumor is pressing against the brain and how much it has started to intertwine with it."

I loved the idea of getting my arm and my leg back. Then maybe I could do the monkey bars with Lexi. Maybe I could run as fast as Cassie and the other girls. And maybe I could act out parts of *Romeo and Juliet* without my weird arm gestures.

My parents asked more questions, and the doctor answered. But one question really got my attention. "Is it cancerous?" Mom asked. I wasn't 100% sure what cancer was, but I knew it was always serious.

"We don't know yet," Dr. Montoya said. "Usually, these kind of tumors aren't. We'll have to biopsy it and send it to the lab after the surgery. But it's the tumor itself that is the concern right now because it's pressing against the brain."

The doctor paused, looking at both my parents for a few more seconds, then she squatted down and looked me in the eye. "Do *you* have any questions, Maddie?"

For some reason, having a neurosurgeon staring at me made me uncomfortable. But I nodded. "What . . ." I didn't quite know how to ask what I wanted to ask. "What could go wrong?"

Mom and Dad shared a look. Maybe they had wanted to ask that question when I wasn't around.

"Good question," the doctor said. "Most of my surgeries go very well, but there is a chance that we won't get all the tumor," she explained. "And then we'll have to watch it to make sure it doesn't grow back or spread to anywhere else."

So this whole thing might not be over very quickly.

"And there is a chance the surgery or the tumor might do damage to your optical nerves, and you might lose some sight."

I didn't like that either. I really liked being able to see.

"And in some cases, those who have had the surgery have some side effects with their brain. For example, it could damage the part of the brain that tells you when your stomach is full when you eat. If that part gets damaged, then you'll probably gain a lot of weight. There are some possible behavioral changes, too. Some patients have had parts of their personalities change." She said it all in a normal tone like she was talking about the weather or what she was going to have for dinner.

I think my mom nearly burst into tears on that one. Maybe she didn't want me to change. I didn't want me to change either.

My dad reached out his hand, like he was going to stop the doctor, but then lowered it. Dr. Montoya didn't hold back. And maybe my dad decided that was okay for me to hear.

"If it is cancerous and has spread to other parts of your body," Dr. Montoya continued, "we may also have to do some radiation. And because the radiation is so close to your mind, it may affect it. It may be harder to learn."

I didn't like this list. In fact, I super-ultra-mega hated it. My brain could get messed up, my personality could change, it might be harder for me to learn—and there was more?

"And because it's on the pituitary gland, that gland may stop functioning. So you may have to take medication to supply the hormones your body needs."

"How long would she need to take the medications?" my dad asked.

"The rest of her life," Dr. Montoya said.

The rest of my life? Wow. Bad wow.

Dr. Montoya opened her mouth again. There was more? She looked down at me. "And there is a very slight chance we might lose you. It's possible with every surgery, no matter who the surgeon is. That shouldn't happen. It is only if something in the surgery goes terribly wrong, but we are dealing with a very important part of your body."

I might die.

For some reason, hearing the doctor say it felt so much heavier than anything before. It made the monster feel even more real. More dangerous.

I forced a smile. It was probably a painted smile like I'd seen Cassie do. One I didn't really feel.

"Tell her again what could go right," Mom said, trying to help out.

"Well," Dr. Montoya said, "we could get all the tumor, and if it didn't spread and isn't cancerous, you never have to worry about this again. We never know until we get in there."

"And they will do their best," Dad said.

"And when do we do this?" I asked.

"Two weeks," Dr. Montoya said.

"Wait," I said. "And would I be better two weeks after that? I'm in a play." We were going to perform in four weeks.

The doctor looked back at me. "It's possible," she said. "You will probably be out of the hospital after a week, but it will take several weeks before you're really up and moving."

"Can we change the surgery?" I asked, looking at the doctor and then at my mom and dad. "Do it after the play?" My mom and dad looked to the doctor.

"I wouldn't recommend it," Dr. Montoya said. "I'm really busy, and this spot just opened up. If we postpone the surgery, it might be another five weeks or so, and I don't want you to wait that long. The tumor probably isn't growing fast, but it is growing, putting pressure on your brain, and you're losing your motor skills. I think we'd better stick with the date."

So maybe I only had two weeks to live.

And if I did live, I probably wouldn't get to be Juliet.

# CHAPTER 19

# Shakes

I shoved a huge spoonful of cookie dough shake into my mouth. It helped. A lot. And because it was a Shane's Shake Shack shake—say that ten times fast—it was big. There was no way I was going to finish it, but I could put it in the freezer when we got home and eat the rest another day.

Before we went to see the neurosurgeon, Mom had promised me a shake afterwards. Something to look forward to.

"Do you have any more questions about what we heard?" Dad asked, scooping another spoonful of his eggnog shake.

I know. Eggnog. Weird. Maybe brain problems run in my family.

"No," I said quietly. I had lots of questions, but I wasn't sure I wanted to hear the answers.

"Maddie, listen to me for a second," Mom said. She had a mint chocolate chip shake. She had much better taste. "Because this is a crazy time, you might find yourself thinking a lot about what is scary about it, what could go wrong, and what you're missing. But to be fair, you need to also think about everything that could go right. You have to at least give the good as much thought as the bad."

That made sense.

"Yeah," Dad said. "It's not that we need to ignore the bad, but we don't have to worry too much about what could happen until we know what will happen. That way we don't waste any energy on stuff we may never have to worry about."

I nodded.

"It's like being in the dark," Mom said. "Have you ever been scared in the dark because you imagined that something was going to get you? Nothing bad was really there, and you freaked yourself out for nothing."

I had done that so many times. I used to imagine a monster with twenty-seven arms, googly eyes, and a laugh like my twin brothers'. Trust me. It was creepy.

Mom patted my hand. "You can't waste your energy being worried about something that might not be real."

She was right. I shouldn't worry too much about the really bad stuff because it might not happen. But the tumor did seem like a monster ready to pounce, something with terrible gaping jaws and jagged scales all over its body. I shook my head. Here I was worrying while my mom was trying to teach me not to worry.

"When I was a kid and scared of the dark," Dad said, "I used to imagine I knew a supernatural martial art that could take down monsters. I could kung fu vampires, ghosts, zombies . . . you name it." Now you know where I got my imagination from. "I imagined myself winning any battle I needed to fight. I even practiced my moves right before bed sometimes, just to make everything clear to any monsters watching."

I envisioned my dad practicing made-up karate moves, and I couldn't keep my laugh in. Mom couldn't either.

"I was little," he justified, "but it helped me not be scared."

"I want to see some of these moves," Mom teased.

Dad raised his arms in a kung fu pose, then playfully fake-punched my mom's shoulder. "It's silly. I know. But it worked."

I smiled. I could definitely do that.

"But," my dad said, "there were times when I was so scared I couldn't control my imagination. That's when I tried Secret Number Two."

"What was that?" Mom and I both asked at the same time.

"I prayed," he said. And that was it. He didn't preach some sermon or tell any story. He just said he prayed.

We talked some more; it was mostly my parents trying to make sure I kept my spirits up. And it worked. I knew they loved me. I knew it before tonight, but a Shane's Shake Shack shake and the talk sealed it again.

"There is something we have to decide," my mom said. "When do we tell people?" Oh, yeah. I was kind of hoping to avoid that. "I think it should be soon. People will want to help and support you."

I still didn't like the idea, but I guess it had to happen. "Alright," I said. "You can tell people."

"Including your teacher?"

I nearly choked on my shake. If she told Mrs. Baer then Mrs. Baer would probably want to tell the class. And then the whole school would know. And then she might take Juliet away from me. Maybe Cassie would get the part, and I would end up as Juliet's nurse. Or maybe I wouldn't have a part at all.

But I couldn't see any way around it. I swallowed then took a deep breath. "Yeah."

# CHAPTER 20

# Telling the Class

"I talked to your mom," Mrs. Baer said. She had called me to her desk as soon as I came in. She rested her hand on my hands. I had been wringing them in front of me. "I'm really sorry to hear your news. Do you want to talk about it?"

I didn't feel like I had anything to say, but I liked that she asked me.

Mrs. Baer gave me a sympathetic smile. "Just know that you can always talk to me, okay?" She was really nice. I think she had a super teacher heart. "How do you feel about telling the rest of the class?"

I sighed and looked behind me. Mrs. Baer always said you should face problems and not just ignore them, so this didn't surprise me. Most of the kids were working on their vocabulary worksheet, but Cassie was watching us. She didn't smile when I caught her eye. In fact, her neatly trimmed eyebrows scrunched together in the middle of her forehead.

I shrugged back at Mrs. Baer.

"I think we should tell them," Mrs. Baer said. "So they can help you. We all want to support you. You have lots of friends here, Maddie."

That last sentence surprised me. Why would she think I had lots of friends? I had spent my share of recesses sitting against the wall with nobody to hang out with. Of course, I did walk home with Yasmin, and now I was hanging out with Lexi more, so maybe that's what Mrs. Baer was talking about.

"If you don't want me to, I won't," she said.

"It's okay," I said. "You can tell them."

Mrs. Baer nodded. "Actually, what do you think about telling them yourself?"

Me, telling the whole class about some crazy tumor in my head? I shook my head. I think I would rather jump out of a plane strapped to bowling balls and land in a lake of boiling acid.

Mrs. Baer said she could do the talking. "But would you stand up in front of the class with me?"

I shook my head again. I didn't want to. Plus, I thought it would be better to be ready to make a fast dash to the hall if the class freaked out.

She waited until it was almost time for recess then stood up in front of the class and called for attention. Everyone quieted down and looked up from their worksheets. "If you didn't finish your vocabulary then it will be homework," she said. Even though she was super nice, Mrs. Baer still gave homework. "But before recess, we have one more thing to talk about. By raise of hands, who has faced something scary before?"

A "monster lurking in the darkness" scary.

Several hands went up.

"Can you give me some examples?" Mrs. Baer asked before calling on a few people to share. Yasmin talked about being in a car accident. Just hearing about it made me nervous. Tori talked about going on the Haunted Mill ride. That thing is creepy, especially the skeleton that pops out of nowhere at the end. Seriously, I almost jumped onto my brother's head the first time I rode that ride. And Jackson said that he had a neighbor who smelled like cats and was always trying to give him hugs. Not as creepy, but the whole class laughed. I wanted to, but I was a bit jumbly inside.

"Well," Mrs. Baer said, "someone in our class is facing something that is pretty scary." She pointed at me, and everyone turned.

I wouldn't have minded the attention if I had just received the high score on a math test or been recognized as the funniest girl in the world for my creative use of mustaches, but this was different. Very different.

"Maddie went to the doctor," Mrs. Baer continued, "and they found a tumor in her head. They are going to have to do a surgery to try to get it out so it doesn't hurt her brain or her eyes." She paused for a moment to let that sink in.

I held my breath, but nobody screamed in horror. Not one kid. A few gave tiny gasps and had sad looks. Others didn't seem to understand.

"It's important to know," Mrs. Baer said, "that there are great doctors who are going to help her, but also that this may be a really difficult time for . . ." She didn't finish. Her voice got all choked up, like she was trying not to cry. Almost immediately little drops of tears started to gather in the corner of my eyes. No fair. I didn't know it would be crying time. Part of me hated that this was happening, and the other part loved that Mrs. Baer cared enough to cry. I didn't know teachers did that.

The room got all serious. That happens when someone cries.

Mrs. Baer wiped her eyes. "Sorry," she said. "It's just hard to see a sweet little girl go through something so hard." No one was wiggling. No one was teasing or laughing. "And I thought you should know. We need to be very supportive of Maddie."

Some kids had glossy eyes like they might cry, too, and others were nodding. Lexi brushed away a tear. After a moment, Robin's hand rose up in the air. "My dad had a surgery on his knee. He said that the doctors used tubes to go in and fix stuff. Is that what they are going to do with Maddie, but in her head?"

Everyone looked at Mrs. Baer and then to me. "I believe so," Mrs. Baer said, still sniffling.

Two more hands went up.

"Will she get to eat as much ice cream as she wants after the surgery?"

Mrs. Baer looked at me, and I nodded.

"That's good," Devin said.

"Will she have to wear those hospital clothes that don't have a back and people might see your underwear?" Cesar asked.

Everyone laughed. I kind of did, too. "I hope not," I said.

They laughed again. Maybe because it was funny, or maybe because they wanted a break from the serious stuff.

"Will you have any brain damage?" Coby asked.

I didn't have any jokes for that one. I didn't know what to say. It was on my worry list. Dr. Montoya told me we wouldn't know until after the surgery.

"She'll be fine," Mrs. Baer said, saving me from the question.

I hoped she was right. I liked my brain, and I really liked it undamaged.

Lexi reached across our desks and squeezed my arm. I put my hand on top of hers for a second, to say thanks without having to say anything. I wished I had stood up for her one of those days Cassie wouldn't let her hang out.

I looked at the clock. One minute until recess. Almost done.

Cassie raised her hand. "When is her surgery?"

"Two weeks," I said.

"And how long until you're back and feeling okay?" she asked. I could almost see her mind working, the hope in her eyes. And her hope was against me.

"I'm not sure," I said. I didn't want to mention that it could be a few more weeks. I didn't want her to know.

"If she's not back, do you think I could be Juliet?" Cassie asked Mrs. Baer.

Really? We had just announced that I had a tumor and it was scary and serious, and she was trying to get my part?

Mrs. Baer didn't smile. "We aren't going to worry about that right now."

And then the bell rang.

But I was worried about it right now. I was worried about it all.

# CHAPTER 21

# Another Mission

As I shuffled toward the door to go to recess, I must have been really nervous; my weird hand fisted really tight, causing my nails to dig into my palm. I pried the fingers loose with my other hand.

Cassie looked at me out of the corner of her eye. I wasn't even going to ask if I could hang out with her anymore.

I had only made it a couple of feet when Yasmin met me. "Maddie, I'm so sorry." She gave me a big hug. I hugged back.

"Are you okay?" Lexi asked. She was right behind me.

I nodded.

Devin walked by and smiled, then he waved quickly and

grabbed a basketball. Cesar did a lesser version of the same thing. Neither one of them had ever done that before.

Yasmin, Lexi, and I started to walk out into the hall. Yasmin tried to help me like I was super sick or weak or something. She had her arm out to catch me if I started to fall.

When we walked outside, Coby was waiting. "Is it like cancer?" he asked.

"We don't think so," I answered, "but we don't know yet." More kids gathered.

"Are you scared?" Sailor asked.

I shrugged. I was terrified, but I wasn't going to break down in front of everyone.

"Sorry, no more questions," Cassie said, cutting through the crowd with a huge smile on her face. "Maddie is hanging out with me." She took me by the hand and pulled me away from the group. "We need a little friend time." And then we walked away.

Friend time? Really? That was so different from what I thought she would say. I thought she hated me. Well, maybe she still did, but she was being nice because there was a chance that she could get Juliet back. Cassie didn't invite anyone else to hang out with us, just us two. That was strange and kind of cool. Or was it? I really didn't know.

"So, how are you, Cassie?" I asked. I was uncomfortable with too much silence as we walked.

"I'm always good," she said. "I'm so sorry you have a

problem in your head." She sounded sincere, but it was a lot like the voice she used around adults.

"I guess it's okay," I said.

"Does it hurt?" she asked.

"Not really. But it's why my arm and my leg don't work very well. My eyes are a bit blurry too."

"Oh," Cassie said. Then she shook her head. "I'm sorry."

We walked for a little while without talking. That didn't usually happen with Cassie. "I don't know much about tumors," Cassie said, "but maybe I could help with something else."

Help? Cassie was going to help me? She didn't hate me?

"I know," Cassie said, throwing both her arms in the air. "I could help you with your crush." She nearly bounced as she walked. "I think you know mine is Devin. Who's yours?"

"Umm," I stalled. I didn't really have one. Well, not really. "I'm not sure."

"I was thinking like Jackson or Coby," Cassie said.

"Maybe," I said. But sometimes I still wanted to drop Coby in the Pacific Ocean.

"We could plan a way to get their attention," Cassie said. My mom and dad said I shouldn't even think about having a boyfriend until I'm older, and since I'm only twelve, I have a ways to go. But I could probably try to get someone's attention.

We started walking around the playground. "Do you know

what?" Cassie said. "Maybe what we should do is plan how I can get Devin's attention and that will help us know how to get Jackson's or Coby's attention later."

That kind of made sense.

"What do you know about him?" Cassie asked.

Devin? I knew he liked basketball, that he had a little brother clone named Sam, that he liked Star Wars stuff, that he was embarrassed to play Romeo but liked it with a mustache, and that I thought he had a crush on Lexi. But I didn't tell Cassie the last part. She asked me several more questions, and I tried my best to answer them.

"I know," she said, her voice rising. "Maybe we should invite them over for a swim party. All of them. I have a pool in my backyard, you know."

I knew. Cassie had said that lots of times. She also had a condo in Hawaii. "Why don't you ask Devin if he could come this Friday. And then if he can, we'll invite Coby and Jackson, too."

I nodded. I love to swim. My dad calls me a fish. My mom calls me a torpedo. I just call me awesome.

"Okay," she said. "Thanks. I think we should probably work on this fast. Would you mind asking Devin?"

"I can do that," I said. Cassie thanked me, and I started walking away toward the basketball court.

Wait. Cassie had done her magic again. She had kindly asked me to do a favor for her, but if it didn't turn out well again, she would probably be mean. Again. And this was just after she found out I had a tumor.

What if it didn't go perfectly? I had enough to worry about. But I did kind of want to. Maybe I should just do it. I could imagine it was like gathering an elite team of superheroes for some world-saving mission. Or maybe I was rounding up the best cowboy gang to free a town being held captive by marauders.

Or . . .

I slowed down. I didn't need any more stress. Getting friends together should be fun for me, and if it wasn't, I shouldn't do it. And I didn't have to do everything Cassie said.

I turned and walked back to Cassie. She was catwalking back to gather up some more girls. "Wait," I said. Cassie looked at me. I think she was a little surprised. "I think we should invite Yasmin, too." Then it would be a lot more fun.

Yep. I actually did it. This wasn't my imagination. I'd actually walked back to Cassie and asked if I could invite Yasmin.

"Sure," Cassie said.

Wow. That worked out just fine.

I almost turned and left again, but another idea had been swimming in my head. I took a deep breath and then it just came out. "And Lexi." Yep. I actually said it. "I think she would really like it," I added quickly before I didn't have the guts anymore.

What had gotten into me?

Maybe it was because I had to worry about tumors and hospitals and dying that standing up to Cassie wasn't as big of a deal. Or maybe the tumor was giving me superpowers or something. Maybe it was releasing the part of my brain that was afraid of stuff because I was doing things I had never done before.

Cassie stared at me.

Oh, no. She was going to blow up at me.

"I don't think that's the best idea for the party," Cassie said.

That wasn't a blowup. I looked at Cassie for a moment, and then I did something different. Maybe I was feeling stronger because my first tries had gone well. Or maybe my tumor was still giving me superhuman courage. I almost put my hands on my hips. "I really think we should," I said. I forced myself to look Cassie in the eyes.

I really *really* wanted to look away, but I didn't.

Cassie looked at me. No smile. "Okay, but I'll invite her," she said.

Wow. It worked. And Cassie was going to invite her? That would be perfect. Maybe they could become friends again. This idea of being a little braver was working.

"Perfect," I said. "And I'll ask Devin later today when we have play practice."

For a moment, Cassie's smile faded. "Okay," she said.

And I was off on another mission. A swim party mission.

# CHAPTER 22

~

# Murder, Death, and Talking to a Boy

I pretended to be looking out from a tall balcony over a courtyard at night, saying my lines to no one in particular.

Juliet was talking to herself. I liked that. I talk to myself sometimes. But Juliet was talking about Romeo. Awkward, but sweet. I don't talk to myself about my crush. I mean, I don't even have one. So I don't . . .

Well, you get the point.

And I was talking with a mustache on.

This time, before we even started practicing, I offered a red curly mustache to Devin and he took it. I had a thin blue one.

"'Tis but thy name that is my enemy," I said. "Thou art thyself, though not a Montague." My lines were confusing, but I had to know all about the play to understand them. Juliet wished Romeo had a different last name. It wasn't that she didn't like it. He didn't have a really weird last name like McStinketh or Nerdworth. It was Montague. And it wasn't the actual name that was the problem but his family. The Montagues were enemies of Juliet's family, the Capulets. Juliet wished Romeo wasn't a Montague so she could marry him and not have to worry about her family beating him up, or egging his house, or throwing her in the loony bin for liking him.

"What's in a name?" I asked, continuing my lines. "That which we call a rose by any other name would smell as sweet."

I think that means that it doesn't really matter if you call it a rose or not, it's still a really pretty flower and smells good. In modern times, I might have said something like, "Even if you call brownies something else, they are still amazingly tasty." But I don't think Shakespeare ever had brownies. If he had, he definitely would have mentioned them, because . . . brownies.

"I take thee at thy word," Devin said.

As soon as he spoke, I jumped. I was supposed to. And I was trying to be a good actress. Juliet had no idea Romeo was there, listening in the dark. I thought it was kind of creepy that he was sneaking onto Juliet's property, but he was a cute stalker. Plus, while we practiced, Romeo was a cute stalker in a curly red mustache.

"I love how you act like I scared you," Devin said. "It's fun. Most of the other plays look like they'll be boring." He glanced around at everyone else practicing in the other corners of the room.

"Thanks," I said, smoothing over my blue 'stache. "I can't wait for my line when I tell you to go away before someone finds you and murders you." I wished I was wearing the curly mustache so I could twist it like a villain in a cartoon.

"But they aren't going to catch me," he said like he was the fastest person on the planet. "I'm not dying today."

"But you do eventually die." I didn't really think about the words before they came out of my mouth. But they were true. Romeo is handsome and super flirty, but he dies at the end of the play. And we had to do that scene too. I didn't like that. Death wasn't exactly my favorite subject right now.

"You okay?" Devin asked. I guess maybe my smile had disappeared.

"Yeah," I said. "I just don't like the ending. I don't think I want to perform it."

"I know," Devin said. "Talk about depressing."

And apparently Shakespeare thought Romeo's death wasn't enough. Juliet is fun and lovable and talked to herself and all that, but she dies too. Neither one of them gets their happily ever after. It's part of what makes them famous. But I didn't want to be like Juliet, and I didn't want Devin to be like Romeo.

"I think the ending is supposed to be a lesson for people

not to fight with each other," I said, "but they could probably get that across without us dying."

"Probably," Devin said. His face was different. I wasn't really sure what his expression was, but his face was a little squinched. "Maybe we should pretend they don't die in the end of our play."

I almost jumped right out of my mustache. Cheese tots, that was brilliant! "I nominate that as the best idea I've ever heard from someone wearing a red mustache," I said.

Devin laughed and rubbed his red curly 'stache.

"But maybe," I said, "we should take it one step further. Maybe we should make up a different ending."

Devin nodded.

"Okay, let me think." I tapped the forefinger of my good hand against my temple just to put out the thinking vibe. At the end of the play, Juliet fakes her death, but Romeo thinks she is dead for real and is so upset he takes poison. I know—super downer, Shakespeare. "After Romeo poisons himself, I think Juliet should pull out an antidote. Then he wakes up, they both twist their mustaches, give each other a high five, and then they start dancing."

"Dancing?"

"Yeah," I said. And then I did a little shakey-shakey. "And a disco ball comes down from the ceiling, and everyone in the whole show starts dancing together and singing, just like in a music video." I didn't do my most amazing moves, like spinning on the floor, but I did do the wave and a little robot. I bet Juliet would have loved to do the robot. It was a little tricky with my bad arm and leg, but I managed.

"That's definitely better," Devin said.

"A *lot* better," I said, doing a spin move to finish off my dance.

"I hope you are back in time to do the play," Devin blurted out. "It's a lot more fun to practice with you than it would be with Cassie." He turned red for a second. Not as red as his mustache, but still pretty red. "I'm not saying she's mean or anything. It's just that you bring mustaches and it's fun and stuff."

That made my insides feel all creamy, like mashed potatoes. "Thanks," I said. "I think you're fun, too. Some people would never wear my crazy mustaches."

"Like Cassie?"

"There is no way she would wear one," I said. "Well, maybe if it was sparkly and matched her shirt."

We both laughed at that.

"And speaking of Cassie," I said. "She's having a pool party and wanted me to invite you." I was kind of surprised how easy the words came out.

"Me?" he asked, pointing at himself.

I nodded.

He scratched the side of his head. "Are *you* going?"

I nodded again. Why did he ask that? Not that it was bad.

"Will there be any other boys?"

"I know she's going to invite some," I said, "and Yasmin and Lexi are coming." I threw Lexi in there just to sweeten the deal.

He didn't turn red this time. Maybe he was getting used to talking about girls. "Well," he said, "if my parents say I can go and there are a couple of other boys from the class then I'll come."

I wanted to twist my mustache again, but not like a villain. Like a happy, mustache-wearing girl. This was going to work.

# CHAPTER 23

# Swim Party

"Cannonball!" Coby yelled and jumped off the diving board. When he hit water, waves shot out in every direction, soaking everyone. Cassie squealed and jumped out of the pool so the water wouldn't mess up her hair. I had just come up for air and let all the water hit me in the face. It was just water. No biggie.

All the boys Cassie had invited came. Well, not Jake. He was out of town visiting his grandpa or something. But Devin was there, and after he agreed to come then four other boys said they would come. They were splashing each other like crazy.

Seriously, boys are weird. It was like a contest to see who

could get the others the wettest. But, hello, they were all in a pool. They were already soaking.

I swam over to Yasmin.

"You okay?" she asked.

I guess I wasn't swimming very well. "Yep," I said. "Except for my left side got bit by some raging beast of the sea, like a killer whale or something."

"Oh, is that all?" Yasmin asked. "You sure have to deal with a lot of monsters." She was probably remembering the Dragoporkisaur, but it made me think of the real monster I was going to have to face soon.

"Have you seen Lexi?" I asked, changing the subject. She had left me another card in my backpack telling me how sorry she was to hear the news about my tumor. That made me super glad I stuck up for her.

"No," Yasmin said. "Not yet." She looked around the pool.

"I hope she gets here soon."

Yasmin pursed her lips for a moment. "Are you sure she was invited?"

"Yeah," I said. "Cassie said she would do it herself."

Yasmin raised an eyebrow.

All of a sudden I felt sick. Would Cassie say she was going to invite Lexi and not do it?

The boys splashed us again, and Yasmin screamed and swam away. I took it in the face. Again.

"Are you guys all having a good time?" Cassie's mom asked.

She had just stepped out from the big sliding glass door on the deck wearing a satiny dress and high heels. Her makeup looked like it had taken her hours to do and her hair hours more. She walked down the stairs like she was a model on a runway. "I put out some snacks by the pool if you want them. But don't eat until after you're done swimming. You don't want to get cramps."

"Thanks," I said. A few of the other kids followed my lead.

"Cassie," her mom called out. "Come here for a second." Once she got to the bottom of the stairs, she was closest to my end of the pool. I started to see how long I could tread water. I had done it for like fifteen minutes straight before. Of course, that was before my arm and leg started acting all weird, but I tried anyway.

It took three more calls before Cassie came over, and when she did, she looked embarrassed and bothered. "Not now, Mom."

"Not now, what?" her mom said. With all the boys splashing and a lot of them on the other side of the pool, I was probably the only one who could hear the conversation. "I'm doing you a huge favor by having this party. You know we shouldn't."

I didn't know what that meant. Why shouldn't they have a party?

Cassie huffed. "Yeah, I know."

"And you didn't take out the garbage yet," her mom said, her voice not all nice anymore. It was sharp, like an ax.

"That was Dad's job," Cassie said.

"Well, he isn't around, is he?" Cassie's mom was whispering, but it felt like she was yelling. Where was Cassie's dad? She hadn't mentioned him lately. "And you said you'd pick which doll goes online," her mom said.

I wasn't sure what that meant either.

"I know," Cassie said, looking around. It was like she didn't want us to hear. I turned the other direction. I started to swim away, but I was still really curious, so I went slow.

"I'm trusting you. You have to get at least fifty dollars for it, like the last one."

"I know," Cassie repeated.

"Now, garbage, quick."

"Okay. Okay."

It only took a minute before I heard my name. "Hey, Maddie," Cassie said. "Come help me with something." She had probably noticed that I was closest. I turned. Did she know I'd been listening? Even if she did, I wanted to tell her no. Though I was curious about what I had just heard, I wasn't sure if I should be mad at her yet. Getting the garbage wasn't the worst job, and it would give me a chance to ask her if she had invited Lexi or not. If she hadn't invited Lexi I'd be ticked.

"Okay," I said.

Once I was out of the water, I remembered that my

swimsuit was getting faded and small. In the water, it was probably less noticeable. But now that I was walking next to Cassie, whose suit had a frilly skirt attached and matching straps, I'm sure it looked ridiculous. Cassie's must have been a new trend. The tropical colors were bright, and it looked like it was from a movie or something.

Soon we were circling the house by the garage, leaving a trail of drips from the pool. "My mom is making me grab the garbage," she said. "Moms can be so crazy."

I really wanted to ask why Cassie shouldn't be throwing the party, why she had to get fifty dollars for a doll, and where her dad was, but I didn't.

"Yeah," I said. "But your mom seems nice."

"Not really," Cassie said. She grabbed one handle of the garbage can, and I grabbed the other. "We have to end the party right at seven thirty because she has a date with some guy who drives a Hummer." Somewhere in my brain I knew what a Hummer was, but I kept picturing some guy driving a car that was actually humming. But why would Cassie's mom be going on a date, anyway? Where was Cassie's dad? Oh, had he gone? Like divorce-gone? Or separated?

We pulled the garbage down the walkway, which was lined with all sorts of fun plants. It really was a pretty yard. "She went on a date last weekend," Cassie said, "but Mom said he wasn't worth the trouble."

I wondered what it would be like to live in Cassie's home,

where you shouldn't have parties, your dad wasn't around, your mom had dates with humming guys, and you had to get fifty dollars for dolls. I think I would really miss my dad.

But I still had a question to ask. A question that was bothering me. "Hey, Cassie," I said. "Is Lexi coming?"

Yep. I asked it. I was growing braver and braver all the time.

Cassie looked at me for a moment. "I don't think so. She said she had to do something else."

"But you invited her, right?"

I asked that one too.

She smiled. "Of course." She sounded convincing, but I didn't know if I believed her. We had pulled the garbage a few feet away from the snacks. "That's good," she said, brushed her hands off, and led the way back to the pool. When we got there, she jumped into the water.

I was going to ask Lexi on Monday and find out the truth. And if Cassie hadn't asked her, I was going to be super-steam-coming-out-the-top-of-my-head mad. But if Cassie had asked her, I was being upset for no reason. I didn't know how to feel.

I was glad to get back into the pool. I swam back toward Yasmin.

"Let's race," Coby said, probably louder than he needed to. "Like a relay. Boys against girls."

Everyone quickly agreed, and we all started lining up. Some of the boys even started to stretch, like they were getting into show-off mode. They thought they were all hotshots, but they were going to go down.

"Wait," Cassie said. "Maybe let's have a few sit out."

"Why?" Cody asked.

"Like, maybe Maddie doesn't want to go," Cassie said.

"I'll go," I said, swimming closer.

"Yeah, but," Cassie said, and pointed. They were all watching me swim. All of a sudden, every move I made felt super awkward. I tried really hard to use my left arm, but I was pretty sure it wasn't working.

"It's because of the tumor," I explained, "but I like to pretend that a giant orca bit my left side, and I'm trying to swim to safety." I stopped and treaded water. "And there it is." I pointed behind Cassie at Coby. "It's a huge killer whale, and it's going to bite your toes right off. Get out of there!" I screamed the last part and everyone dove into the water to swim away.

Coby totally played along. Everyone was swimming away from him, splashing and laughing, and he chased after them.

"And it's not just any orca," I yelled. "It's the dreaded Orcalops, the one-eyed monstrosity of the deep."

Devin and a few others laughed at that, and Coby even closed one eye. He was slapping his arms out in front of him like they were giant jaws. And he almost had Hannah.

"That's not funny, Maddie," Cassie said.

"I thought it was funny," Jackson said.

"Me too," Devin said.

I liked having the boys around. Maybe they weren't so weird.

"I mean, it was funny," Cassie said quickly, like she'd changed her mind for some reason. "It just surprised me."

"That's why it was funny," Devin said, talking louder over all the splashing.

Cassie smiled big, but then looked at me. I could tell her eyes were on fire and she was super upset with me. She swam closer.

"You are ruining my party," she whisper-yelled at me, just like her mom had done to her.

How could I be ruining the party when everyone was having fun? Plus, I wasn't sure I trusted Cassie right now. I really wished Lexi had come. I think she would have liked my game. And the boys reacted so well to my jokes.

"Maybe I'm not ruining your party," I said. And I actually said it. I looked at everyone else. "Watch out for Orcalops!" I pointed at Coby again.

Almost immediately he smiled and raised his arms to look like giant jaws.

Cassie glared at me.

I smiled back.

## CHAPTER 24

# Poison Dragon Death Claw

"Did Cassie invite you to her swim party?" I asked Lexi as we walked out of Mrs. Baer's class for our first recess. I had wanted to ask her sooner, but her bus had been late to school.

Lexi looked at me, confused, for a few moments. "No," she said. "Why?"

No.

And not only had Cassie *not* invited Lexi, but she had lied to my face telling me that she had. Oh, I was mad. Yep. Steam-popping-out-of-my-head mad. Cassie used me and then lied to me. Now I was glad I hadn't listened to her and kept playing Orcalops.

"I told her that she should invite you to a swim party," I said to Lexi. "And she told me she would."

Lexi smiled. That seemed weird while I was so mad. "That's so sweet of you." Then she shrugged. "But I'm not surprised Cassie didn't come through."

Something inside me clicked. I didn't really care anymore if Cassie liked me. Not at all. My surgery was coming up, and I didn't know how long I would be around. And I didn't want to be part of her games anymore.

"C'mon," I said, grabbing Lexi's hand. I pulled her right over to where Cassie was walking around the path with several other girls. Lexi pulled back a little. I could tell she didn't want to go, but I was pretty determined.

"We're a little busy," Cassie said before I even opened my mouth. She could probably tell I was upset. "Maybe in a little—"

"Maybe now," I said. This wasn't in my imagination or anything. True story. "I came over to say that I've been hanging out with Lexi more and more since you haven't been letting me hang out with you, and she's awesome. And I want to play with her whenever I can. She's super fun. We already survived crossing the Sahara together." I got some weird looks at that, but they were followed by smiles. Especially by Yasmin. "Anyone who wants to come hang out with us is welcome. And today we're trying out something new and awesome. It's a game." I didn't even know what I was saying, but I was mad and I wanted to make sure I invited everyone to do something other than get wrapped up in Cassie's lies and tricks. I had to make up a game name fast, and it had to sound good. "It's called Poison Dragon Death Claw," I said. Not bad.

"What is that?" Hannah asked.

"You can come over to find out," I said. Was I stupid? Was this all a strange symptom of my tumor? Well, maybe it was okay. Maybe someone needed to stand up to Cassie.

"I'll play," Yasmin said. "I love Maddie's weird imagination." She took a step toward us.

My heart pounded faster. It was actually working. I looked at the other girls.

Nope.

No one else came. Maybe they thought they were too mature for a game. Maybe they only wanted to walk and talk. Or maybe they were all trying to impress Cassie. But having Yasmin with me made it feel like a victory. So Lexi and Yasmin and I walked over to stand under the biggest pine tree. I looked back over my shoulder, and yep, Cassie was definitely watching us as her group continued on the path. She wasn't staring all the time, but I caught her glancing over more than once.

"Okay," I said, "this is how you play the game." I didn't really know what I was going to say. But before I started, I saw some fifth graders passing by. "Hey, guys," I waved them down. "Do you want to play Poison Dragon Death Claw with us?" They looked at each other for a moment. "It's super fun. Try it."

Thankfully, they agreed. Whatever the game I was about to make up, with Cassie watching, it would look better with more people playing. "Okay, so I'm the dragon." Yeah. That was a good start. "I go to the middle between this tree and that one." I pointed across the field. Ideas were coming to my mind just a second before I said them. I was really glad I had practiced using my imagination a lot. "And you guys have all come into my lair to rescue the prince I took captive."

"Don't dragons usually capture princesses?" one of the fifth graders asked.

"Nope," I said. "Most dragons like princes better. It's a little-known fact." I smiled.

One of the fifth graders looked at me like I was describing how to watch television or eat chicken nuggets.

"Anyway, I like to give people who come into my lair a chance before I eat them or touch them with my poison claw." I raised my finger like it was a claw. "So I'll give you a category, like colors or seasons or kinds of pizza."

"Pizza?" Yasmin said.

"Yep," I said. "Most dragons love pizza—another little-known fact. They like princes and pizza. And then all of you have to think of something in that category. So if it was pizza, you could think of pepperoni pizza, or Hawaiian, or the works."

"Okay, then what?" Lexi said.

"Then I start guessing types of pizza. If I guess yours, you have to try to get to the other tree. If you make it without me touching you, you're safe and I won't eat you. But that means everyone else has to try to make it to that side as well. And if I touch any of you with my poison claw"—I wiggled my finger—"then you become a dragon, too, and you have to help me get everyone else."

Yasmin clapped. "Okay, let's start." I was pretty sure she was acting extra excited because she was my friend, but I was grateful for it.

"Let's start with pizzas," I said and waited until everyone had picked one. "Barbeque Chicken," I called out. No one ran. "Pepperoni," I said. One of the fifth graders ran toward the other side of the field. She was faster than I thought she would be. Plus, I was slower. She made it. Then everyone else made it. No one got Poison Dragon Death Clawed. I didn't really even come close.

But they were all smiles.

After three more rounds, I finally tagged Lexi. I think she let me. But then we got everyone else.

Then Lexi had to start as the dragon. We played a few more rounds until the bell.

I was so glad everyone was laughing and talking as we went back into class. I knew Cassie was watching.

# CHAPTER 25

# Over the World

Mountains passed beneath me. Pyramids. The ocean. And I felt the movement of going up over the peaks and down by the water. Locked in and holding tight, I was hang gliding over the Great Wall of China.

And this wasn't my imagination.

Okay, just a little bit.

It was a ride in Disneyland. Well, actually in California Adventure, the other Disney park close to Disneyland. I sat in this chair that moved in front of a giant screen, and it totally felt like I was flying over different parts of the world.

Awesome.

I went from ride to ride with my family. Then, in the

afternoon, my parents let me and Christopher go off together, ride whatever we wanted, and meet back for dinner. Everyone was so happy, and my dad took all sorts of pictures: me with Christopher, me with Daisy Duck, me with the twins both sticking out their tongues, me with some princesses, me and my mom eating Dole Whips.

Mmm. Dole Whips.

Sooner than I wanted, we were back in the condo we had rented, crashing for the night. At least we still had two more days of the vacation. Away from school. Away from problems with Cassie. And especially away from neurosurgeons.

But even with all the running around all day, I couldn't fall asleep. And even with all the good memories I'd just made, I kept thinking about my tumor. I lay in my bed and tried to think about anything else. Tried to make myself fall asleep. Tried not to worry about the monster coming for me. Had it gotten bigger? Sprouted spikes like ax blades down its spine?

No. I didn't want to think about it.

I tried to sleep for a long time.

Maybe during the surgery, the doctors would tap into a special part of my brain that would give me superpowers for real. Like I'd be able to move stuff with my mind and see the future.

Or maybe I wouldn't.

I yawned, but didn't feel close at all to actually falling asleep. I thought about my friends. I reviewed all of my lines as Juliet. Then I tried to remember all of Romeo's lines, too. I pictured Devin in different colored mustaches.

And then my door opened. I made sure my eyes were closed. I didn't want my parents knowing that I wasn't sleeping. I peeked the tiniest bit through my eyelashes. There was just enough light coming in from the hallway that I could see.

My dad. He had probably been staying up late, trying to get his work done. At this point, the book was ready, but he had to work on marketing. He was answering questions for interviews and doing a bunch of social media stuff to help people find out about his book.

I don't think he was planning on sleeping much. But with all the work he had to do, why was he in my bedroom?

He stood over me for a second and knelt down beside my bed. He lightly put his hand on my arm. I could tell he was trying not to wake me.

And then he bowed his head.

He was like that for a long time.

A really long time.

My heart filled. If it was one of those huge reservoirs, it was overflowing, flooding over.

And he stayed there.

I was starting to wonder if he had fallen asleep when he sniffled. A few minutes later, he stood up. Then he slowly left the room.

I put my hand where my dad's head had been. Wet. Tears.

I know it's going to sound stupid, but I put my finger in it and then touched my head. Maybe that was it. Maybe they were magic tears and could heal my tumor. Maybe they would work.

"Can't sleep?" I heard my mom ask.

I was busted.

Wait. Nope. She was talking to my dad. "Just getting some more work done," he said. He had left the door open between our rooms, so I could hear them pretty well.

"Well, this vacation is fantastic," Mom said. "Everyone is having a great time."

"Yeah," Dad said. "Now we just need my book to do well so I can actually pay for it."

I didn't realize that we didn't really have the money for the trip.

"But it's worth it," my mom said. "We need this."

"I agree," he said. "And even if something goes wrong, we'll have good memories and a lot of pictures."

Though my heart was still full like a reservoir, it grew stormy and wavy. That's why he'd been taking so many pictures—in case I died or I got brain damage or something. That way they could remember this good time. Remember me. I hadn't even thought of that.

"Do you . . ." my mom started to say, but then stopped. She took in a deep breath and then started again. "Do you worry much that we might lose her?"

My dad sniffled. "Yeah. I've got to believe that good stuff is coming, that we will be blessed, but I worry. All the time." For some reason, hearing that my mom and dad were worried hurt a little. They had taught me so often that I had to think about the good, the positive, but in a strange way, it also helped to hear that they were scared, too. It felt normal. At least a little.

"I wake up sometimes," Mom said, "when you go into her room. Do you do that every night?"

"Every night," he whispered back. I had no idea. I guess there were lots of little tear puddles that had happened that I hadn't noticed. "I just like to see her. Make sure she's okay. It's a lot for a little girl to handle." He sniffled. "And I pray."

"Me too," Mom said. "Me too."

"I don't know what I'll do if we lose her." My dad's voice was soft.

I felt squishy inside. Really squishy. And terrified.

Even Disneyland wasn't going to fix that.

# CHAPTER 26

# The Basket and the Big Lie

"Here you go," I said and gave Lexi a card. Then Yasmin. Then lots of others. I had made a bunch of cards on the long car ride home from Disneyland. On the front of the card was a little black mustache on a pink piece of paper. Above the mustache was the letter *I*, and beneath it were the words *you a question*. Get it? *I "mustache" you a question*. Pretty awesome, huh? I didn't make it up, though. It's written on one of the magnets I have.

On the inside of the card, I wrote, *How did I ever get as good of a friend as you?* That was the question I needed to ask. That part I did make up. Then I signed it.

On some of the cards I wrote an extra line or two. On

Yasmin's I wrote, *Thanks for walking home with me and making me laugh, and helping me defeat the Dragoporkisaur. And thanks for coming to play Poison Dragon Death Claw with me. You're the best.*

And on Lexi's I wrote, *Thanks for crossing the Sahara with me. Thanks for distracting the basketball boys. And thanks for giving me cards. They made me feel so good I thought I should give all my friends one. I'm copying your great idea. I'm really glad we became friends.*

"Thanks, Maddie," Lexi said after she read her card. She hugged me super tight. I hugged her back super tight. She was smiling more lately. Maybe I had kind of helped her out, but I knew that she had helped me.

I glanced back and saw Cassie walking with Hannah behind us. She had been watching very closely as I had delivered my cards. I was pretty sure she wanted one. She didn't like being left out of anything. But I hadn't made one for her. I was still really mad that she'd lied to me at the swim party.

The bell had rung. I had just finished my last recess before the surgery, and my little group of friends still played the game I'd made up. Yasmin and Lexi were there, plus Sailor. She had heard what Cassie did and started playing with us. Oh, and there were a few more fifth graders, too. It was really fun. The last round, the runners had to pick flavors of ice cream. I picked potato flavored.

Just kidding. I like potatoes, but potato ice cream would be disgusting. I picked cookie dough.

As we walked toward the school, Yasmin gave me a hug. And Sailor.

I slowed as we got closer to our room, hoping that Cassie and Hannah would separate a little. Finally, after we walked through the doorway, they started in two different directions toward their desks.

"Hey, Hannah," I said, reaching out my hand with the card in it. "I made this for you."

Hannah looked down at the card, then back at me. "No, thank you. Not after your big lie."

What was she talking about?

"Okay, students. Recess is over," Mrs. Baer said. "Back to your seats."

I moved to my seat, but I was still trying to figure out what Hannah had said. I hadn't lied about anything.

Mrs. Baer taught us about geography, specifically tundras. That made me cold. But the fact that I still had another card besides Hannah's that I had to deliver made me nervous enough to warm me up. I wondered if this was going to be my last day of school. Ever.

I hoped not, but I wasn't going to do any homework.

"And today you only have twenty minutes to practice your plays," Mrs. Baer said, "because I'll need a few minutes before the bell."

I got up and moved to the corner of the room where Devin and I always practiced. I reached out with the same curly red mustache. Devin took it, slapped it on his face, and spouted off a few lines. He was trying a little too hard, but I laughed anyway.

When it was time for my lines, I didn't bother. "Keep it," I said.

"What?"

I pointed at his mustache.

"Oh. Thanks," he said then cleared his throat. "I mean, deepest gratitude to you, good Juliet."

I think I may have blushed. "You're most welcome, Romeo."

"Seriously, thanks," he said.

"Sure. If Cassie takes over as Juliet, wear it just to freak her out a little, okay?"

"Definitely," he said.

"Shall we continue?" I asked and slapped on my own mustache.

He nodded and we jumped in. It seemed like the time passed really fast. I think we were getting better. With our lines memorized, we could focus on where we moved and making everything as funny and cheesy as possible.

I really wanted to do this scene for everyone—especially the anti-death scene Devin and I had made up. Nobody was going to die on my watch. Not Romeo. And, I hoped, not Juliet.

"Alright," Mrs. Baer said. "Time to come back to your seats."

It was now or never. I held out a card to Devin.

"Two gifts?" he asked.

I nodded, and he said thanks again. "Remember," he said. "We agreed there wouldn't be any dying." He said it like he had practiced it, but at the end, his voice went a little different.

I nodded and tried to smile.

"Please go back to your seats," Mrs. Baer repeated. A minute later, she continued, "There are only about five minutes before the bell rings, and we have something very special to do." And then Mrs. Baer looked right at me. "Maddie, will you please come up to the front of the classroom?"

"Um. Sure." Sixty eyes looked at me as I walked to the front of the room. What was going on?

"Anyone want to say anything to Maddie?" Mrs. Baer asked. And lots of kids said a lot of things.

"Good luck tomorrow."

"I hope everything goes great for you."

"You're really brave."

"I hope you get lots of ice cream and Jell-O at the hospital."

Mrs. Baer thanked the class and then put her hand on my shoulder. "We have something to give you." She nodded at Lexi and Yasmin, and they went behind Mrs. Baer's desk. They came out again with a huge gift basket. I mean, like you could fit at least two basketballs in there.

"This is from our whole class," Lexi said.

"We all brought whatever we wanted to give you," Yasmin said.

I think my face was confused because my mouth wanted to smile, but my eyes wanted to cry. I blinked hard and tried to focus on the smiling. The basket was full of stuff. Some of it was all wrapped up. Some of it wasn't. I could see crafts, pajamas, fuzzy blankets, a stuffed penguin, nail polish, sparkly slippers, and soda pop–flavored ChapStick.

Maybe Mrs. Baer was right when she had said that I should tell my class because I had a lot of friends.

"Thank you very much," I said, and the tears came even though I didn't want them to. Then Mrs. Baer's eyes thought it might be a good idea to cry too, even though her mouth was smiling. So did Lexi's and Yasmin's. I thought maybe Devin's eyes did, too, but it was probably just a weird glint in his eye.

I liked the stuff, but I liked the people more. And I could wrap myself in a fuzzy blanket and remember them. Or I could use some soda pop–flavored ChapStick and think of them.

I looked out at the rest of the class but noticed some of them weren't teary. That was okay, but they looked upset or confused. There were even a few scowls.

Cassie raised her hand, and Mrs. Baer called on her. "I heard that Maddie made this whole thing up and that she doesn't really have a tumor and she doesn't really need surgery. She just wants attention."

What? Was that the lie Hannah thought I told? Why would I ever make up something like this? I shook my head.

"Cassie, that's not appropriate," Mrs. Baer said. "Maddie definitely didn't make this up. This is a very real challenge she is facing." She opened her mouth to say more, but the bell rang, and all the students got up and left. Mrs. Baer repeated that I hadn't made it up as they exited.

I stood there with a giant basket full of gifts, wondering if my class regretted giving it to me. Thanks to Cassie, some of them thought I'd made the whole thing up.

# CHAPTER 27

—⌓—

# Made It All Up

"What's in there?" Ethan asked, coming to sit by me. He never sat so close to me, especially not in the van on the way home from school. He had seen my basket. My mom had been at school to pick me up so I didn't have to walk everything home. She'd known about the basket and told them the kind of stuff I liked.

"Can I see?" Emery chimed in, moving next to me on the other side.

"Can I have some of it?" Ethan asked, grabbing the plush penguin off the top. I tried to protect my things, but the basket was hard to guard from every side. And since Christopher went to junior high, he wasn't in the van to help me keep back the twins.

"Ooooh, this ChapStick smells like soda." He started to open up the ChapStick and paused to smell it.

"Gross! Don't put that on your lips," I nearly screamed. My twin brothers have germs that can't be found any place else on earth. I had to be careful. I didn't want my stuff to get all grossified.

"How many stuffed animals did you get? One. Two. Three—"

"Please don't touch those," I said, knowing my brothers wouldn't listen or follow what I said. "I'll count them later."

"This blanket is really soft." Ethan rubbed it against his cheek.

And then Ethan said something I never expected. "I wish I had a brain tumor."

I froze.

Why?

Why would he ever say that?

He must not be thinking right at all.

"You do not want a brain tumor," Mom said, and she was using her "listen to me now" voice.

"Yes, I do," Ethan said back.

"Maybe you want a bunch of neat presents," Mom said over her shoulder while turning the van into our neighborhood, "but you don't want all of the hard things Maddie has had to go through and will continue to go through. Count your blessings that you are healthy, and see if there is a way you can help Maddie."

"Nobody ever gives me presents like this," he said.

We pulled into our driveway. We don't live that far away from the school.

"Yes, they do," I said. "On your birthday and on Christmas and sometimes—"

"Not on a *Monday*!" he yelled and stormed out of the van and into the house.

Mom took a deep breath and turned to follow him.

"Mom," I said before she left. "He has my soda pop ChapStick in his hand."

Mom nodded. "I'll get it back." Then she looked at me. "What's wrong?"

She must have seen it on my face. Moms can see lots of stuff on their kids' faces, like a bit of chocolate or a paint smudge from art class, but also when something's wrong.

"Um . . . a girl at school told everyone I made up everything about my tumor to get attention."

"Really?" Mom said. She asked a few more questions to be sure I wasn't overreacting. Then she exhaled slow and long. "That's not nice at all. Why do you think she did that?"

"I don't know," I said. And I didn't.

"I don't know either," Mom said. "But if I had to guess, I'd say that there is a good chance she is feeling a little like your brother. Maybe she's jealous of all your attention but doesn't realize all the hard things that come with it."

"Maybe," I said.

"Do you want me to call her parents or your teacher?" Mom asked.

"No," I said. That would make things worse. I told her it would be okay and took the basket into my room.

I started to read through the cards my classmates had written for me. Even the kids who didn't know me that well, like Enzo and Jade, wrote nice things. I wondered if they still meant them after what Cassie said.

Devin's card got my attention. Like a typical boy, he didn't write much:

> *Dear Maddie,*
>
> *I hope everything goes really well in the surgery. You're awesome. Thanks for being a great Juliet and bringing mustaches. I like you.*
>
> DEVIN

I read it again. He didn't mean he *liked* me, liked me, did he? He liked Lexi. I thought back through every time I saw him blush. Was he blushing because of Lexi or could it be because of . . . ?

No.

Maybe.

Why would he like the short girl who can't run as fast as everyone else and holds her arm weird?

Even if he did like me, he probably didn't like me anymore.

I thought about that note a lot.

Then I read Lexi's. She had given me a little stuffed rabbit with something special. Yep, a pink mustache glued on under the rabbit's nose. Definitely funnier with a mustache.

> *Maddie,*
>
> *I don't know if you know it, but you've been my best friend. Thanks so much for talking to me and playing with me. I thought this rabbit was super cute, and I hope you love him. But I also thought he would need a mustache to be good enough for you. I hope he makes you smile whenever you see him.*
>
> *Lexi*

I hoped Lexi didn't believe Cassie. It was hard enough to go through surgery without thinking I might have lost some friends, too.

Then I read Cassie's note. I didn't think she would have written one. After all, I hadn't given her a card.

> *Maddie,*
>
> *When I first met you, you were very sweet and nice. But then you changed. You*

*started being mean. You stole my part in*
*the play. You ruined my party. You just*
*want all the attention. That's probably*
*why you're talking about the tumor the*
*whole time. I bet you made it all up.*

Cassie

After I read it, I wished she hadn't written it. I wondered if Cassie hoped I would die.

# CHAPTER 28

# Dear Mom and Dad

*Dear Mom and Dad,*

*I'm supposed to be sleeping, but I can't. I tried, but it didn't work. I ended up staring at the glowing green stars on my ceiling for a long time. Thanks, Dad, for helping me put them up after Yasmin gave them to me in my basket. I don't know why they are green, though. Somebody at the glow-in-the-dark factory should have probably spent more time actually outside looking at stars.*

*I'm nervous and hungry. Why do I have to go without food before surgery? Boo. I have to* go in for brain surgery _and_ skip breakfast tomorrow? I just can't catch a break.

I worry about a lot of stuff. What am I going to be like this time tomorrow? Is my tumor going to be gone? Will my brain be all messed up? Will I be able to see well? Will my arm and leg work right? Will I look different?

I especially worry that I might not get another breakfast.

Ever.

Boo.

Super boo.

I would really miss pancakes. And hash browns. Definitely hash browns.

And lots more.

I would miss all my friends. If I don't make it, please tell them all that I love them. And give them lots of hugs from me.

Lots and lots. Especially Lexi and Yasmin.

I'll miss Mrs. Baer, too. Please tell her thanks. Thanks for the basket. And thanks for caring more than any teacher ever.

And tell my brothers I love them. I really do. Even the twins. Give them hugs, and a few kisses right on their faces. I know they don't like that. But I do love them.

*And I love you!! Thanks for everything. Thanks for teaching me to imagine. Thanks for helping me with the doctors. Thanks for telling me everything's okay. Thanks for giving me mustaches because they make me laugh. I put one of them on the bottom of this letter to make you smile if I don't make it.*

*If I do make it, I might tear up this letter before you ever get to read it.*

*I do super love you. I will miss you so bad. So bad.*

*Dad, I hope your book goes really well. I hope I can be there to see it on the shelf in the bookstore. I woke up one night when you were praying for me. That made my heart stronger. Thanks.*

*Mom, I know you pray for me, too. I say my own prayers, and I said a good long one tonight. I prayed to be back with you when all of this is over.*

*I love you forever,*
Maddie

# CHAPTER 29

# 4:45 AM

My parents woke me really early. Like four forty-five early. Seriously, no one should ever be up at that time, especially when they haven't slept very well before that. Today was the day I had to face the monster. I had to look into those burning eyes and hopefully survive. We grabbed our bags and drove the two hours to the children's hospital. I fell asleep twice.

It all felt like a dream. Was this really happening? We checked in, and a nurse led us back to a room and handed me hospital pajamas with rocket ships on them. They gave me yellow socks. They weren't fuzzy, but at least they were a good color.

Oh, and my hospital pajamas had pants so I didn't have to worry about my underwear showing. That was a relief.

"Hello, Maddie," the nurse said. He smiled a lot and had cars on his hospital clothes. They weren't as cool as rocket ships. He checked a lot of stuff, like my temperature and whatever that thing that puffed up on my arm measures. Oh yeah, blood pressure. Then he looked at his watch. "Okay, time to go." He reached into the hall and pulled a wheelchair into the room. "You might not have expected this, but you get a ride to the surgery room."

Ride in a wheelchair? Okay. That was kind of fun.

He pushed my chair, and Mom and Dad walked next to me. They were trying to talk all normal, telling me to remember all of this so I could write it down later and asking me what I wanted to do when I was all better.

Then the nurse said something I didn't realize. "At the end of this hall, you're going to have to tell your mom and dad good-bye, and I'll take you the rest of the way to the surgery room."

What? I was going into surgery alone?

I always thought I'd be able to go all the way in with my mom and dad. My fingernails dug deeper into my hand.

"We can't go in with her?" Dad asked. Apparently they didn't know about this either.

"No, I'm sorry," the nurse said. "Everything has been sterilized, so you'll have to say good-bye right up there, where the hallway has a red stripe."

My mom grabbed my good hand.

I wanted that stripe to stay far away, like the other side of the world away. Banished to another dimension away. But it didn't. I squeezed my mom's hand.

I hated that stripe. It came up really fast. The nurse stopped my wheelchair.

"You're going to be just fine," Mom said, crouching down right in front of me. She gave me an awesome hug, and it was like I could feel her love from her heart and arms and everything.

"We'll be praying for you," Dad said. He gave me a good hug, too. "You've got this."

All the words were right, but I could see the worry in their eyes. I remembered what they said about losing me. Maybe they were just as scared as I was.

I hoped I would be able to go home to take back that letter on my desk before they found it.

And then the nurse started to push me past the stripe.

Alone.

I tried not to shake.

It would be alright.

"So, what's your favorite color?" the nurse guy asked. He had lots of questions, like where I went to school and what movies I liked. I answered them all, but short and sweet. I was a little stressed-out.

Okay, a *lot* stressed-out.

It would be alright.

He would have done a better job of distracting me if he had been wearing a mustache.

The nurse rolled me right into the surgery room.

It felt more dreamlike than coming to the hospital. This was where they were going to do the actual surgery. Everything would happen right here. The room had several machines, some on rolling stands, and a few people in hospital clothes. They even had masks and gloves on. I didn't see Dr. Montoya. A nice lady in hospital scrubs helped me get on the table and rest my head on a cushion.

"Hello, Maddie," she said. "I'm an anesthesiologist." Wow. Another huge word. It would be worth like seven thousand points in Scrabble. "I'm here to make sure you feel really comfortable. So comfortable that you'll fall asleep and when you wake up everything will be done."

That sounded nice.

"I'll put this mask on you." She showed me a simple mask with a tube attached to it. "You breathe for a little while, and you'll rest through the whole surgery. Now what flavor of gas would you like?"

There were flavors of gas? I had no idea. She read the list, and I chose root beer. I didn't even hesitate. Root beer–flavored anything sounded like a good idea.

She put the mask on my face. "Does that fit okay?"

I nodded. It was weird, but I couldn't imagine a mask ever really feeling natural.

She flipped some switch, and the gas came on. "Now, relax and count to one hundred."

Okay. That wasn't too hard.

*One. Two. Three. Four.*

What was that? Ugh.

Root beer gas was not as delicious as I was hoping.

*Five. Six. Seven.*

I wondered what my parents were thinking.

*Eight. Nine. Ten.*

Seriously. Why did I choose root beer? Yummy soda. Decent ChapStick. Terrible gas.

*Eleven. Twelve.*

I let my eyes rest while I kept counting. I wondered how long . . .

Yawn.

*Thirteen. Fourteen. Fifteen.*

I knew I was going out.

*Sixteen. Seventeen. Eighteen.*

And then they would send tubes up my mouth and under my nose to my brain.

*Nineteen. Twenty . . .*

I couldn't fight it anymore. I was falling asleep hard.

I just hoped I would wake up again.

## CHAPTER 30

# A Tower of Dinosaurs

I was bound mummy-style and carried above the heads of chanting island natives. They were carrying me on a long staff with my hands and feet tied to it. They were chanting in a language I couldn't understand. It kind of sounded like "Banana juice. Banana juice." Which is a really weird thing to chant. Maybe they really liked bananas. But can you make bananas into juice?

The natives set me down in a large open area, and then some lady who looked like a witch doctor with messy hair and a necklace with animal claws looked right at me. She got closer and closer. And then she shoved something up my nose.

I couldn't see it, but I was sure it was a bone going from one side of my nose to the other, just like in the movies.

Then the ground shook.

It wasn't a huge shake, but I could feel it.

Again.

And again.

Behind the witch doctor lady was something huge. It took a second for it to come into focus.

A brontosaurus.

Yep. A ginormous dinosaur.

The natives chanted louder and louder.

The dinosaur backed up, turning its neck to look behind it.

*Beep. Beep. Beep.*

Did brontosauruses beep? It was like a truck backing up.

And then the dinosaur sat right on my head.

Seriously.

Have you ever had a brontosaurus sit on your head? I didn't think so, but it did not feel good. The pressure was crazy. I thought my head would squish down like potatoes being mashed.

And then another brontosaurus stepped up. I could barely see it, but I guess one of my eyes wasn't covered by the other big dinosaur bum.

There was more beeping, but this dinosaur wasn't walking backward. It climbed on top of the other one. Now I had two dinosaurs on my head.

More and more dinosaurs came until I had a tower of seven brontosauruses sitting on my head.

One of the natives grabbed my hand and whispered. Apparently it had learned to speak English because it wasn't asking for banana juice anymore. "Maddie. How are you feeling?"

The chanting quieted down, but not the beeping.

"They say you did a great job."

A great job at what? Letting dinosaurs sit on my face? Well, I didn't want it. I wanted them to get up—now.

Wait.

Dinosaurs didn't usually sit on top of one another. At least I didn't think so. And they didn't make beeping sounds. In fact, there shouldn't be any beeping sounds in the jungle.

Oh.

I wasn't awake. At least, not really.

I opened my eyes just a crack and saw a bunch of blurry stuff.

I felt someone else grab my other hand. "Hey, Maddie. You're okay. You did a great job." This one was a man. "It's all done. And you rocked it."

Rocked it?

My dad.

I opened my eyes more.

Blurry Dad.

Blurry Mom.

I wanted to cry. Double cry. Once because it felt like seven dinosaurs were sitting on my head, and twice because I was alive.

Alive.

I'd made it. I'd been in the monster's gaping jaws and somehow survived.

A hospital room.

Beeping. Somewhere to my right.

Nothing was chanting "Banana juice." That was just a crazy dream.

My eyes closed again, but I noticed it was hard to breathe. I tried again. I could do it, but it wasn't easy. Probably because of the bone the witch doctor had put through my nose.

"Rest as much as you want," Mom said.

I wanted to open my eyes again, but I was still so tired. "I can't breathe very well," I told her.

"You have a bandage in your nose," Dad said, "so you can't breathe through your nose."

Not a bone. A bandage. I reached up and carefully touched the bandage. My face felt sore, but I couldn't tell if that was because of the bandage itself or all of the swelling.

Swelling would explain the head pain, the trouble breathing, and the overall ughs.

"It's called a mustache bandage," my mother said. "We didn't make that up. That's what the doctors and nurses actually call it. You look like you have a mustache."

That was the first thing that even kind of made me want to smile. I ran my finger gently along the bandage. "Can I see it?"

My mom appeared in front of me with a tiny pocket mirror. "It's quite stylish." She was grinning. At least I was pretty sure she was grinning. Her features were still blurry. I adjusted the mirror in her hand, pulling it closer, and saw that I had a large white strip stretched below my nose.

A mustache bandage.

I kind of wanted to smile again, but I was way too tired and achy.

"Hey, Maddie." A new voice. I glanced to the side. Dr. Montoya. "The surgery went very well." She put her hand on my hand. "Let me just check a few things. Can you look straight forward for me?" Dr. Montoya waved a tiny flashlight in my eyes.

"Brownies," I said.

"I'm sorry, what?" She put the flashlight away.

"I want mashed potatoes and brownies."

All of a sudden I was really hungry, and everyone had told me that after the surgery I could eat whatever I wanted.

Dr. Montoya laughed. "We'll talk about that in a minute." She lifted my pajamas just enough to look at my stomach. Could she tell that I was hungry that way?

She poked my stomach. "Does this hurt?"

It wasn't comfortable. Then again, when is somebody

poking you in the stomach comfortable? I shrugged, but only a little. I still didn't feel like moving a lot.

"How is your scar?"

I had a scar?

She touched a part of my stomach that hurt. I yelped.

"It will be a little tender for a while, but it's healing properly."

That's right. I had a scar on my stomach. It was where they pulled the fat tissue from. Suddenly the idea that there was tummy fat inside of my head almost made me lose my appetite for brownies.

Almost.

"Mashed potatoes and brownies," I repeated.

"I'm sorry," Dr. Montoya said. "No solid foods until the mustache bandage comes out."

What? No one said anything about that before. That was just mean. How could they deny mashed potatoes and a brownie to a kid who just got cut open, put back together, and had dinosaurs stacked on her head?

"Do you want some juice?" Dad asked. "Apple? Grape? Orange?"

Dr. Montoya whispered to Mom and left.

This all seemed familiar. "Was I awake before?" I asked.

"Yes," my mom said. "Don't worry. It's tough to remember."

"And did you offer me juice?"

My dad nodded. Maybe my parents offering me juice was why the natives were chanting. But what was the deal with banana juice? I finally agreed to grape juice and gave it a few sips.

"Did they get the tumor out?" I asked. Dr. Montoya said the surgery had gone great.

"Most of it," my dad said. "Like ninety percent."

"They left a part of it attached to your hypothalamus because they didn't want to damage your brain," Mom said, putting away the mirror.

"Good," I said, not sure if that really was good or not. All I knew was that it didn't sound like they'd damaged my brain and I wanted to be asleep.

I was so glad they got most of the tumor.

But they didn't get it all, and I wasn't really sure what that meant.

# CHAPTER 31

## Mustaches

I was floating right up out of my chair. I looked down and saw my hospital room. Mom and Dad were there. My dad was sleeping on the couch, and my mom was resting next to my bed in a chair.

But I didn't have any control.

"Mom, why am I flying?"

"What did you say?" She rubbed her eyes.

"Mom, I don't want to fly." I was going to float right up through the ceiling and then out of the hospital. Was I dying?

My mom jolted up and grabbed my hand. "You're okay, Maddie."

"No. I'm not. I'm flying away."

"You're not flying. You're right here, safe in your hospital bed."

"No. I'm not." I could imagine just about anything, but this wasn't my imagination.

"Yes, you are," my mom said. "What you're seeing isn't real. You haven't slept for almost four days, and the doctors say that might be causing you to hallucinate. I need you to calm down and relax."

Calm down? I was floating, maybe dying. But my mom said I was okay, and I trust her.

I trust her.

I'm okay.

Four days without sleep. I could remember it now. I know that sounds crazy, but I just couldn't sleep. Between the doctors and nurses popping in, the pain, the light and noise of the busy hospital, having to go to physical therapy, and how slowly I walked and ate and moved, I'd hardly closed my eyes. Plus, there was the worry. I'd had a crazy surgery, but they didn't get all the tumor. They didn't know what would happen next. Maybe the rest of the tumor would die. But maybe it would grow back. Maybe I would have to do this all again. And if I did, it would be more dangerous the second time.

"The doctor said that sometimes patients in the Intensive Care Unit have trouble sleeping," Mom said. "Your body has just been through something really hard and is still under a lot of the stress that comes with recovering. And without that important rest, you can start to see things that aren't there."

I tried to close my eyes and relax. I'd definitely add this to my list—the things-that-super-stink-about-my-life-right-now list:

1. My head still felt like dinosaurs were sitting on it. Maybe they were smaller dinosaurs now, but they were still dinos. Medicine helped, but I could only have it every few hours.

2. Hormone problems. *Hormone* is a weird word, but everybody has lots of hormones, and they control lots of different stuff in your body, like your mood, your ability to deal with stress, and even some balance between stuff like water and salt. And apparently my hormones were all whacked out. The doctors and nurses needed to give me medicine every so often so that my body wouldn't shake uncontrollably and hurt itself.

3. My eyes were still blurry. The doctors said they didn't know if that would get better or not. Boo on that. I wanted to see my mom and dad clearly. I wanted to go back to school and see my friends. Not just blurry images of what I thought might be them.

4. Finger pricks. The doctors had to check my blood all the time. That meant finger pricks. I hate finger pricks. A nurse would wipe my tender, beautiful fingertips with a cold alcohol swab then jab them with a needle. That was bad enough, but then they would squeeze my finger to try to make the blood come out. Sometimes they had to squeeze and squeeze, over

and over, to get enough blood. After a few pricks on the same finger, it hurt to touch things. It was awful. And every few hours the nurses were back to poke me again. All day and all night. That also kept me from sleeping.

5. I finally got my mashed potatoes and brownie. I know it doesn't seem like it should be on my list of bad stuff, but it was. Because when I saw that potato, all mashed and buttery, and that brownie, all chocolaty with a thick frosting and a thin layer of mint underneath, I got excited. Finally something good was going to happen. But then I took my first bite. Guess what? It tasted like nothing. I could have been eating broccoli and it would have tasted the same.

I cried.

I know it sounds silly after going through neurosurgery and having huge headaches and getting pricked all the time, but I had really been looking forward to those potatoes and that brownie. The doctors said my sense of taste should come back in a couple of days, but what if they were wrong?

Back to the list.

Where was I? Oh, yeah. Number six.

6. I still had some of the tumor in my head. I know I talked about it before, but it's on the list again. It's also numbers 7 through 28. Boo on the tumor. It was like the monster could come back even though I'd beaten it. Sure it was smaller, but was it dead? Its eyes weren't roaring fires anymore, but lit match heads. Its spikey spine was bumpy like the small teeth

of a zipper. It wasn't nearly as threatening, but would it grow back? Bigger? Stronger? Apparently monsters could do that.

29. My friends might not even think any of this was real. They might think I only wanted attention, and they either aren't thinking about me now or are super mad at me.

30. I didn't know if I would be better in time to be Juliet in the play.

31. I was seeing things that weren't there. That actually would explain why I thought my dad was pushing me in a wheelchair to his friend's house where we saw horses but then ended up in physical therapy on the third floor. I hadn't really wondered about the horses until now.

The good list was shorter:

1. I was alive. I like being alive.

2. The doctors took out most of the tumor. That was definitely good.

3. I was getting the use of my arm and leg back. Yep. Maybe I'd be able to catch someone if we played Poison Dragon Death Claw again. That was, if my friends let me play.

4. My brain seemed like it was okay. No damage the doctors could see.

5. Maybe I'd be able to taste mashed potatoes and a brownie soon.

My dad was snoring on the couch. Why couldn't I sleep like him?

"I'm going to insist they get you stronger medicine to sleep," my mom said, "but first I want to show you something."

"What?" I asked.

My mom opened her laptop and booted it up. I tried to blink away the blurriness in my eyes, and it helped a little. She typed in a few things and waited. "Can you see my screen?"

I nodded.

"You really need to see it," she said. "Scoot over." She motioned with her hand, and I slowly moved over. Mom laid down right in my hospital bed with me. I really liked that. It was like she was a patient with me. "Check this out," she said. "Your friend Yasmin sent me some pictures."

Yasmin? At first I was relieved, but then I wondered if these were good pictures or pictures of her sticking her tongue out at me with a sign saying she didn't want to be friends anymore.

Mom typed in a few more things on her email account, and then there was a picture of Yasmin wearing the mustache I gave her.

She sent that.

She thought of me.

I wanted to smile again. I also kind of wanted to cry. I missed her.

"And that's not all," my mom said. She scrolled down.

Lexi, wearing a purple mustache. Her thumbs were up.

Lexi had done it too. I *loved* Lexi, and her purple mustache was awesome.

"Yasmin must have talked to others at school, and her parents, and some adults got involved. And . . ."

My mom scrolled more, and there was a picture of Sailor with a mustache drawn on the side of her index finger. She held that finger below her nose.

And then Devin. In one picture, he was wearing the mustache I'd given him. But in the next picture, he wore a big bushy black mustache he'd made out of paper. And he was winking.

I liked his winking.

And my mom scrolled some more.

There were pictures of like twenty kids from school, all wearing mustaches.

And then Mrs. Baer. She looked the silliest. I think a real smile crossed my face.

They believed me. They'd sent me messages. They were trying to make me smile.

My mom kept scrolling. There were Devin's parents and Yasmin's parents. The janitor. Mr. Reeve, my teacher from last year. The lunch ladies. Even the principal. And they were all wearing mustaches—for me.

And they all looked hilarious. Seriously, imagine your principal with a blue mustache.

"And," my mom said while clicking to a different screen, "we thought it was a good idea." There was a picture of my dad holding his phone up to his face. He had drawn a mustache on the screen. My mom had one she had cut out from some paper at the hospital. They must have done them while I was trying to relax. They looked pretty hilarious.

And then there were my grandma and grandpa. Both sets. All wearing mustaches. Yep. Grandparents with fake mustaches.

My aunts and uncles and cousins. Even some neighbors.

Then there were some of my nurses. My mom or dad must have told them about it while I wasn't paying attention, which probably wasn't hard when I was hallucinating.

"Yasmin's mom helped her post it online too." My mom switched tabs on the computer screen. There was a picture of Yasmin with a mustache again. Beneath it were the words: "My friend Maddie had brain surgery, and I thought we might be able to make her laugh and let her know we were thinking of her by posting pictures of ourselves in mustaches and tagging them #MustachesForMaddie. That way she doesn't miss any of the silliness."

I felt all full and squishy at the same time.

"A lot of us reposted it," Mom said. "I put them all here." She opened another file. I saw a lot of people I knew, but a lot I didn't. There were people with their kids, all wearing mustaches. Some people even had their dolls wearing mustaches. Or their dogs. Seriously, dogs with mustaches. That made me laugh right out loud. One guy put a giant mustache on his car. Another guy made a mustache out of toothpaste. Gross, but awesome. There was even my dad's editor and everyone at the publishing house, all with mustaches.

"There are over four hundred of them," my mom said. "People love you."

"Four hundred?" I asked, trying to wrap my mind around that many people.

"Over four hundred people trying to cheer up one little girl in the hospital." She scrolled through picture after picture. My favorites were the one of a guy who had a real mustache he had grown two inches off his face on both sides and the one of my dad's assistant with a curly mustache she'd made out of fuzzy pipe cleaners. Incredible. And the more I looked at the silly pictures, the less I thought about tasteless brownies, painful finger pricks, or heavy dinosaurs sitting on my head.

And I laughed.

Yep. It came out and I meant it. And it felt good. Well, it kind of hurt my head, but it felt good in my heart.

I looked through a lot of the pictures. Each one made feel a little better. People cared. And they cared enough to take hilarious pictures, maybe even embarrassing ones. It was all to make me smile.

I yawned.

Maybe the smiles had brought the yawns with them.

"I want to rest, Mom," I said.

Mom nodded and hugged me.

With her still next to me in my hospital bed, I finally went to sleep.

# CHAPTER 32

# A More Important Dream, New Toothbrushes, and Cancer

Dad pulled out his phone. "Your brothers want to video chat again. Should we do that?" There was a hospital policy that wouldn't let my brothers come see me. I guess there was too much sickness going around and little kids brought in more.

"Sure," I said. I had actually really missed my brothers. Weird, I know, but true. And by the way they acted the first couple of times we chatted, I think they missed me, too. Of course, I was on some pretty heavy medications when we talked before so I didn't remember much of what we said.

But I knew this was a distraction. Dr. Montoya was

supposed to come visit, and she'd have the results of the test on my tumor. We were going to find out if it was cancerous.

Dad sat on the bed next to me and pushed a few buttons on his phone.

Aunt Kimmie answered the phone with a big smile. She was taking care of my brothers while Mom and Dad and me were in the hospital. "Maddie, I'm so happy to see you." She was extra excited. She asked me a lot of questions and told me she loved me. She's nice like that. "Should I get your brothers so you can talk to them?"

I nodded, but before she actually left, the twins popped their heads in front of Kimmie's. They fought with one another for screen space, and the camera was way too close to their faces.

"Who are you talking to? Maddie?" They both smiled super huge. "Maddie!"

I almost cried. Yep, they were the same annoying brothers, and I still almost cried.

And then the questions began. Ethan tilted his head. "Why do you still look weird?"

Maybe I wasn't so happy to see them.

Just kidding.

I didn't like the idea that I looked weird, though. I didn't look at myself much in the mirror because my hair was always crazy from spending so much time in bed and my face was swollen.

"She doesn't look weird," Mom said. "She's just healing. She'll be back to normal soon."

"I think she looks weird," Emery agreed. They both nodded in consensus, which to them meant it was absolute truth. But that wasn't the end of the stuff they had to say:

"Can you have as much ice cream as you want?"

"Max went in your room and used your markers. I put them away again, but I thought you should know."

"Have you seen all of the mustaches online?"

"We have mustaches too. I'll go get them."

"Yeah. Me too."

I didn't get in another word before they both disappeared. Then Max poked his head into the picture. I've always loved his red hair, but I loved seeing it even more right then. "Hey, Maddie, I miss you."

Melt my heart like butter on a baked potato. "I miss you, too." This time a tear really did escape.

"Are you sad?" he asked.

"No. Just happy to see you."

He thought for a while and then smiled. Christopher poked his head in too. And I cried again. He asked me all sorts of questions to make sure I was okay.

"When you come home we can play Wizard Club," Max said.

"Okay," I said.

"But I don't want to be a dwarf. I want to be a kid wizard who turns into a dragon."

Weird, but I loved it. "Okay."

"But since I'm the littlest, I'll turn into a puppy dragon." Really cute idea.

I could hear the twins coming back as their chipmunk voices got louder. They took the phone.

"These are the mustaches we made for you."

"We taped them to your door, but then we took them off to show you."

"I made this one." Ethan held a large black cowboy-style mustache up to the screen and then taped it to his face.

"I made this one and this one and this one." Emery was showing different colored mustaches too fast for me to really see them. But I had already seen pictures of them online. "When I wear them, I feel like the bad guy in that book with the bandit."

Book? Wait. What was today? "Just a second, guys." I turned to my dad. "Didn't your book come out a couple days ago?"

He gave a tired smile. "Yesterday."

"But you were here with me in the hospital the whole time. You were supposed to go on tour."

His smile didn't leave. "Yep. I had to postpone it." Mom put her hand on Dad's back and massaged it.

"But, Dad—" I was crying. Again.

He waved me off. "There was nowhere else in the world

I would have rather been. I was doing something much more important."

More important.

"But it's your dream," I said through tears. I felt terrible. He had been working toward this for so long. He had stayed up late so many nights.

"You're a more important dream," he said. "And I'm glad I'm right here."

A more important dream.

I still felt a little bad, but a lot super special.

"He's had a lot of friends trying to spread the word for him," Mom said. "They heard about you and knew he was taking care of you here, and they've tried to help out. There are even a few famous authors who heard about Dad and jumped in to let people know."

"Good," I said.

"Um . . . hello?" I looked back down at the phone. Max was waving. "I'm still here."

"Sorry," I said.

He got closer to the screen. "I want to tell you a secret so nobody else can listen." I nodded. "Yesterday, I snuck into the bathroom and licked all of the toothbrushes. And your toothbrush tasted the best."

I could hear a bunch of "eeews" and groans from offscreen. The other boys must have heard. I just started laughing.

Mom leaned into the shot. "Max, can you hand the phone to Aunt Kimmie?"

He did and Mom said, "Kimmie, I'm going to need you to buy new toothbrushes for all of the kids."

A knock hit the door.

"Come in," Dad said while Mom told Kimmie she'd have to call back.

Dr. Montoya stepped into the room. My insides went from super happy to a super nervous mess.

I looked at her closely. I could never tell if she was coming with good news or bad news. Her face didn't show much emotion.

"Hello," she said, looking around the room and then focusing on me. "How are you doing today, Maddie?"

"Fine," I said. Was she asking me how I was doing because I wasn't going to be doing well after she told me the news? Was it cancer?

She asked me a few more questions and then said, "We got your results back from the lab." She took a deep breath.

I hated that breath.

"It's not cancerous."

I think I exhaled bigger than I ever had before. My mom and dad did too.

"That doesn't mean we are out of danger," Dr. Montoya quickly added. I guess she didn't want me to celebrate too much. "We still have to watch it closely. If it grows back, it is still right next to the brain and the optic nerves."

I nodded, but inside I was doing summersaults. No cancer.

"So in a couple of days, I think you should be able to go home," Dr. Montoya said.

Home.

She said *home*.

# CHAPTER 33

# Flushed

No. No. No! Not now. Not today. I could feel it coming, even though I would have done anything to stop it. I made it to the toilet just before I threw up.

Gross.

Icky. Nasty. Bad taste. So gross.

But it was worse than that. Now Mom wouldn't let me go to school. I closed the door.

Flush.

Everything swirled down the toilet, including my hopes.

And then I had to write in my notebook that I'd puked. It's my terrible I'm-going-to-destroy-later notebook.

I had been in the hospital two weeks before I could come

home. And now I had been home for another week resting and taking lots of pills. Seriously, a lot. I had to take pills every few hours and then write down what I'd taken in a notebook. My mom watched to make sure I didn't forget anything.

And it wasn't just that. I had to write down what I ate and drank, when I went to the bathroom, and even if I threw up. Again. Gross. I was definitely going to destroy that notebook later. Who wants a record of how much they sat on the toilet?

We had printed off my favorite pictures of people in mustaches and taped them to my mirror, but that didn't really help today.

I had tried to convince my mom I was good enough to go back to school—just for an hour. The best hour. I had been up and moving, and I'd taken all my pills, and I'd even got dressed nice, but apparently I had been up and moving too much. I didn't feel like dinosaurs sat on my head anymore, just baby rhinos. But baby rhinos still hurt. And if I moved too much or too fast, I got sick. Now, with my head swirly and tired, I wanted to cry, but I think I had used up most of my tears.

Romeo would have a different Juliet in the assembly today.

I was going to have to stay home.

# CHAPTER 34

# Mind Powers

"It's Maddie," Mrs. Baer said and quick-stepped across the room to give me a hug.

Everyone turned in their desks. Lexi and Yasmin ran over and gave me hugs too. Sailor followed. And then Devin and Cesar. They didn't hug me, but they did come over.

"I'm glad you're okay," Devin said.

"Me too," Cesar said.

By now a lot of other kids were standing or had walked toward me. They said lots of things.

"Hey, Maddie."

"I'm glad the surgery worked."

"It's been forever."

"Did you see the picture of me with a mustache?"

They all seemed happy to see me. Except Cassie. She didn't stand up. She had pulled out her phone and was busy looking at the screen and texting something. Lexi had told me that Cassie performed as Juliet, but she still wasn't happy to see me.

My mom was standing behind me holding two trays of cookies with mustaches on them. That gave everyone else an extra reason to be happy to see me.

It had taken almost another week after the play before I finally felt well enough to come back to school, even though I showed up late and was only planning to stay until lunch.

After hugs and questions and mustache cookies, we studied English. That was okay. I was glad to be there and doing something just okay. It's silly what you miss when you're away.

Cassie looked over and glared at me.

Several times.

I guess maybe she was upset that I wasn't gone longer, or sicker, or even dead. Or that her lie had made her look bad. Or that I was getting so much attention and she wasn't.

Finally it was time for recess, but I wasn't going out for long. Maybe a walk and then I'd come back in.

"I'm so glad you're back," Lexi said again as we walked down the hall. I think she had said it like four times already.

"Me too," Yasmin said. We all hugged again, and I thanked them for all the mustaches.

"We still play your game sometimes," Lexi said.

"And when we don't, a lot of the same group still hangs out," Yasmin said. We had left the building and were crossing the blacktop toward the field where we'd first played Poison Dragon Death Claw. A bunch of the fifth graders were waiting for us. I had been part of helping a lot of different people become friends. In fact, I had played a huge part. I'd gotten it started.

I stood just a squoosh bit taller.

"So is your brain all messed up?" I turned around and saw Cassie following us, Hannah by her side.

Wow. Why was she like this? Why would she lie about me having a tumor, be upset and want me to die, and then ask me if my brain was all messed up?

"Kind of," I answered. I saw her sneer increase a little, then falter. Maybe not all of her wanted me to be hurt. "But messed up in a good way. The surgery gave me superpowers. I can see through walls, tell the future, and lift things with my mind." Her sneer dropped.

It felt strange. I was different. None of me really cared what Cassie thought about me anymore. I didn't want to impress her. I didn't feel nervous.

"Whatever," Cassie said.

"Don't be mean," Lexi said. It wasn't loud, but she still said it. Maybe I wasn't the only one who had learned to stand up to Cassie.

"I'll leave you losers to hang out together," Cassie said and started to turn away.

"Hey," I said.

Cassie turned around.

"They aren't losers," I said. "They are two of the best friends anyone could ever have." I did. I said it. It was like the queen had glared at me, threatened to banish me, but I still told her she was wrong.

"Whatever," Cassie repeated and walked away. Hannah looked at us for a moment and then followed.

But Hannah was the only one. Cassie used to have lots of people following her every recess, now she only had Hannah.

"Why don't any of the other girls hang out with her?" I asked.

"Everyone figured out that she was lying about you making the whole tumor thing up," Lexi said. "That was pretty mean. Little by little, no one wanted to hang out with her anymore."

"Can you really lift stuff with your mind?" Yasmin asked.

"Yep," I said. "Look." I pointed toward a tree. "I'm holding up the branches of that tree right now."

"Now *you're* just making stuff up," Lexi said with a smile.

"Careful," I said, "or I'll levitate a bunch of giant water balloons and drop them on you."

"That would be awesome," Yasmin said. "Only it would be better if you dropped them on Cassie."

I smiled big. I liked that idea. If only there was a bunch

of water balloons around waiting to be levitated. And if only I actually had mental superpowers.

The fifth graders came over and talked to me for a while to say they were glad I was better. Then they went back to playing my game. I wasn't quite up for that yet.

By the time Lexi, Yasmin, and I did one lap around the field, I was tired. We had talked about a lot of stuff and I didn't have all the energy I used to. But just before we reached the school, I saw Cassie with Hannah again. It was like we had switched places. Now I was surrounded with friends, and Cassie wandered with only one.

The rest of the day I noticed that hardly anyone talked to Cassie. They didn't want to tell her jokes or hear her opinion. She had lost a lot of friends.

I kind of liked it.

But I also kind of didn't.

In my deepest-down part of me, I didn't.

# CHAPTER 35

# Supernova

"Thirty seconds until we all blow up into teeny tiny pieces!" I yelled, looking down at my watch. If we didn't make it, the entire planet and its three inhabited moons would be destroyed when the star exploded. A supernova would probably look amazing, but we wouldn't be around long enough to appreciate it. Thankfully we had the technology to know when the star would explode and a stabilizer to keep it from blasting apart in the first place.

"We've got this," Devin said. Oh, I mean, Special Agent Vin said into his headset. He raced his space bike through the black sky and stars at superspeed, the stabilizer in his hand. But the robots of Dr. E. Vil were on his tail. Their space bikes were red, with black skulls on them.

Okay. We weren't really in space; we were on the school lawn playing a game I'd made up: Supernova, or Don't Let the Star Explode in Your Face. I hadn't quite decided on an official name yet. One team started with the ball, which was the stabilizer, and tried to get it to the tree at the far end of the field— that was the star about to explode. They only had two minutes, and each player on the team could only take three steps with the ball before they had to pass it. If they couldn't get the ball to the tree in two minutes, or if the other team stole the stabilizer, the other team won.

And the fact that some of the boys were playing with us instead of playing basketball was pretty awesome. The boys had never played with us before. Maybe it was because I invited them and they wanted to be nice to the kid who'd had brain surgery, or maybe my games were actually fun. Maybe it was a little bit of both.

An evil robot veered in front of Vin, cutting him off. Vin turned his thrusters in the other direction and veered to the side. "Catch," Vin yelled into his communicator and hurled the stabilizer through the black.

Cesar—code name Sar—snagged it as he shot by in a jet pack. Seriously awesome. It was quite the pass and catch, but the evil robots weren't backing down. They fired their lasers, chucked their detonators, and flew in pursuit with their matching gear.

We didn't have much time.

Eleven seconds until the star exploded.

*Ten.*

*Nine.*

Sar tossed the stabilizer to Exi, who threw it to Yas. Then it went back to Vin. With each tick, the star came closer to sending us to our annihilation.

*Seven.*

*Six.*

Back to Exi, then Vin. I held my breath. Vin was only feet away, but the evil robots were hot on his trail, and one big robot stood in front.

*Three.*

*Two.*

Vin faked one way on his space bike, then turned the other way, his thrusters sparking and cracking with the power of the change of direction. He almost lost his balance and fell off into space.

*One.*

Vin slammed the stabilizer into the star just as it was about to explode. Tremors quaked through the glowing rock with the terrible force, but then they shuddered down to nothing.

"Saved," I yelled, jumping up and down. "But it was super close."

Devin's team cheered. Yasmin and Lexi gave each other high fives. Devin and Cesar bounced their chests against each other.

I wasn't going to be doing any bouncing just yet. I didn't feel up to it. In fact, I hadn't really played. I was the timer and the first person to throw in the ball. On the bright side, though, I had been feeling good enough to go to school twice this week for the full day. And my game was a success.

"Can I play?" I turned to see a half smile and curly brown hair.

Hannah. She rocked back on her heels while she waited for an answer.

"Sure," I said, having no idea why Hannah had finally left Cassie and wanted to play with us.

Hannah exhaled long.

"Do you want to be one of the good guys trying to keep the star from exploding or one of the bad robots who wants it to explode?" I asked.

"A good guy, for sure," Hannah said. I explained the game and yelled at everyone that Hannah was going to play. Someone said that now the teams wouldn't be fair, but I insisted. It was my game, and anyone who wanted to play got to play. I was tired of people being left out.

"Okay," I yelled, "the star is going to explode in two minutes. Go!" I tossed the ball to a fifth-grade boy who was ready for it. Devin, Cesar, Lexi, and Yasmin were all evil robots now trying to stop the good guys.

I looked over at the playground. If Hannah was here, where was . . . There. In her frilly shirt, sitting under a pine tree. I wasn't sure from this distance, but I thought Cassie was crying. All alone and crying. I don't know what she said or did to Hannah, but now Cassie had lost her final follower. Now *she* was the one all alone.

I glanced down at my watch. "One minute," I yelled at everyone playing.

Cassie was finally getting what she deserved.

But I kind of wished she would just come over and apologize. Plus, I would forgive her. I think something about having to go through a scary surgery and knowing I could die made me not want to hold a grudge. Life seemed too good for that. There were more important things. Plus, I think everyone else would forgive Cassie too. Well, eventually.

But Cassie probably wouldn't apologize.

She sat under the pine tree and cried for the rest of recess.

# CHAPTER 36

## The Surprise Ending

"Lady, by yonder blessed moon I swear," Devin said, his lips moving under an awesome green mustache.

Yep. This was really happening.

"O, swear not by the moon, the inconstant moon," I said, waving my finger a little sassily. It's easier to pretend to be sassy when you're super happy. "That monthly changes in her circled orb, lest that thy love prove likewise variable." Basically Romeo was trying to swear by the moon that he loved me, but I was saying that I thought the moon changed too much to swear by. Juliet was pretty clever, like me.

I would never claim I knew what love was. I mean, I'm twelve. But as far as I could tell, I was in love right now. Deep in love. I didn't know if it would change like the moon, but right now I didn't care. I wasn't in love with Romeo or Devin. I was in love with performing. I actually stood on a stage, doing what I had hoped so bad to be able to do hour after hour while I was lying in bed with dinosaurs or rhinos sitting on my head.

This was real, not just my imagination. I was wearing a beautiful light-blue dress in front of the whole school. And I was wearing a matching blue mustache. There were still giggles through the audience.

Mrs. Baer had arranged for me to be able to do a special performance. It was just for me. To make sure I got to do the part I really wanted even though I had been sick. Mrs. Baer had such a super teacher heart.

We continued our lines, and the audience seemed to like it. Well, as much as they could understand. It was Shakespeare, after all.

As we finished the first scene, everyone clapped for us. I heard my dad call out and my mom whistle. They had said they wouldn't miss the play for anything. My dad was even filming the whole thing on his camera.

Before the last scene, Mrs. Baer came out and explained, "At the end of the play, Juliet takes some medicine that makes her seem dead. And Romeo thinks she is dead."

I quickly lay down and crossed my hands over my chest. That was the death pose I'd seen in the movies. Oh, and I closed my eyes. Otherwise, I would be a pretty terrible pretend dead person. But I wanted to see what was going on so badly, I cracked them open just a little.

My heart beat fast. I knew what was coming.

Devin looked down at me, pretending to discover my dead body. "O my love! My wife!" Yeah, we got married sometime earlier in the play. Not me and Devin, but Romeo and Juliet. I'm *way* too young to be married.

"Death," Devin continued, "that hath sucked the honey of thy breath, hath had no power yet upon thy beauty."

He was basically saying I still looked pretty even though I was dead. I hoped someone had told Shakespeare that was really sweet and sad—and weird. I closed my eyes all the way as Devin finished his speech. When he stopped talking, I peeked again.

He pulled out a bottle with a skull and crossbones on it. Definitely the poison. He drank it. After he pretended to swallow the deadly stuff, he clutched his throat and then fell on his knees. He made gurgling noises for a minute and then toppled forward onto his face. It was an awesome death scene.

And then he just lay there, pretending to be dead.

My turn.

I sat up, coming back to life and brushing off my beautiful dress. After taking in a deep breath, I looked down at Romeo. I tried to wake him, but when he didn't respond, I shook him, pretending not to know he was dead. I think I did a pretty good job of acting desperate and scared. I put my hand to my forehead to really sell it. Then I found the poison bottle in his hand. "What's here? A cup, closed in my true love's hand? Poison, I see, hath been his timeless end."

I pretended to cry. With all the real crying I had been doing over the last month or so, I was pretty well prepared for this part.

But all of a sudden, it wasn't pretend. Real tears came out. I think maybe I had thought too much about death and stuff, and the thought of someone I cared about being dead just made the real tears come. The audience got all quiet.

I wiped my eyes on my fancy dress.

I wasn't sure, but maybe there was a tear in the corner of Devin's eye too.

I knew what Shakespeare thought I was supposed to do next—lose all my hope then find the dagger and kill myself. But I had already decided I wouldn't. I didn't care how sad someone got or how hard life became, I didn't think anyone should ever give up.

We had a plan. The Maddie-and-Devin Ending.

"I will not have thee dying on me," I said. "Especially since you're my friend. Forsooth, we needeth a better ending." The crowd stirred. I'm pretty sure they realized I had changed my lines.

Devin tried not to smile.

I reached into the sash of my dress where I had stashed a green glass bottle. I think it used to hold lemon juice. "Thiseth here is the antidote for your poison." I flipped the bottle around. I had written the word *antidote* as big as I could on the paper I'd taped to the front. "I brought it just in case you were dumbeth enough to drink poison." A few people in the crowd laughed. I liked that. I put the bottle to Devin's lips.

"Come on back to life, my noble Romeo," I said. "My friend," I added quietly.

And he did. He took a deep breath and sat up. He probably came back to life a little too fast, but it was still kind of awesome. I pretended to look surprised and then wrapped my arms around him. It took a second, but then he hugged me back.

I stood, and Devin followed. "And they lived happilieth ever aftereth," I said. "And their parents figured out how to quit fighting like bratty children."

Devin looked at me, and I twisted my mustache.

He twisted his, too, and we high-fived. It didn't feel Shakespearey at all, but I loved it.

Then I pointed offstage, and Lexi hit play on her phone. Some fast dancing music blared out. Yeah, we got permission from Mrs. Baer for that too.

Before I knew it, I was roboting in front of everybody. I just couldn't stop myself. It took Devin a few seconds before he jumped in. He was a little halfhearted at first, but when the crowd cheered, he did a few twisty, almost-break-dancing moves.

Yep. Completely in love with performing.

While doing my happy shakey-shakey, I looked out at my mom and dad. My dad was still filming us and then he scanned the clapping crowd too. So many people were smiling and applauding.

But not everyone.

Not Cassie.

I saw her with her arms folded. I slowed my dancing. She probably didn't like our play for lots of reasons: the mustaches, the changed ending, and the fact she wasn't Juliet.

"You did a great job," Devin said, putting his arm around my shoulder and squeezing. That pretty much stopped the dancing altogether. Then he let go super quick.

"You, too," I said and gave him a light push.

And then someone else was there giving me compliments. And someone else. A few people later, my mom walked up, and I gave her a full-on hug. I used to care if others in my school saw me do that, but I didn't care anymore.

"That was an amazing performance," my dad said, still filming. "You just won the award for the best actress with a mustache."

I put my hand to my chest and pretended I was receiving a trophy. "I'd like to thank all the little people who made my success happen." I pointed to Max holding my mom's leg.

"I am little people," he said, grinning wide.

Then I pointed at my dad and mom. "And all the big people."

"That's right," Dad said and gave me a side squeeze while still filming.

I thought I might watch this video over and over again.

His hug made my head turn a little, and out of the corner of my eye I saw Cassie looking at me again. It was different this time. Not a glare. Not looking down on me. And she didn't seem to be thinking about how she could get me to do what she wanted.

Different.

"Great job," Lexi said, appearing right in front of me. She gave me a hug. Yasmin was right behind her and joined in. We were an awkward three-person hug-blob, and they had blocked my view of Cassie. I tried to soak in the fun and love and forget that look.

But I couldn't.

Even after all the great attention I got, for the rest of the day, I couldn't stop thinking about that look.

# CHAPTER 37

# The Puzzle

I rolled over in bed, trying to fall asleep. I adjusted my pillow and scrunched the blanket between my knees, trying to let my mind wander. Let it help me fall asleep.

I gasped as the evil prince pulled back his bow, the arrow pointed at my heart. All I had to defend myself were my wits, my pretty face, and a small dagger.

"You tried," the prince said. "You tried to expose my plot and take back the kingdom for the rightful heirs. You tried to avenge your father. But you have failed." He was handsome, with long dark hair and a full beard. Handsome, but evil.

I cocked an eyebrow. "Oh, don't get all dramatic," I said with a wink. With my open eye, I carefully watched his fingers holding the arrow against the taut bowstring. I wanted to add something about him being a disgrace to his mustache and how, if I ever got out of this alive, I'd make him shave it off. But that wasn't in the script.

"Try this for dramatic," he said and let go of the arrow.

No more time for thinking. I leaped to the side, pretending to feel the feathers on the arrow brush against my cheek while I made a hilarious "that was too close for comfort" face. It would be an awesome slow-motion shot, with the arrow added in by computers later. The real shot didn't even come close. Oswald, the British guy playing the prince, shot it at least eight feet to my left. We couldn't have any accidents on the set.

Like a ninja, I tossed my dagger at the prince even as I was still falling to the side. Of course it would hit the prince in the heart. Well, they would add the fake dagger sticking out of his chest with makeup in a moment, and I would get to give my revenge speech. They were some of my favorite lines in the whole movie.

"Cut!" the director yelled. "Beautiful, you two. Oswald, well done. Maddie, you're brilliant, funny, beautiful—the works."

"Thank you," I said, not even blushing as I got up off the mattress that had been just out of sight. I did this sort of thing all the time.

"Oh, Maddie!" One of the director's assistants with a clipboard came running in. "You were just nominated for the best comedic actress in the universe for your last role. Congratulations." Everyone on set burst into applause.

"Thank you," I said as I brushed myself off. It wasn't the first time I had been nominated, or even won, but I blushed anyway. I thanked them over and over again as I prepared for my next scene.

And to think that my acting career had all started when I played Juliet in the sixth grade. I had framed the first mustache I'd ever acted in and auctioned it off for thirty-five bazillion dollars for charity.

I smiled as I rolled over in bed again. At least this time I couldn't go to sleep because I was so happy.

I relived performing in front of my school again in my mind. It had really happened. And it had really gone so well, even the changed ending. And so many people had told me I had done a great job.

But that look . . .

Cassie's look kept coming back to me. No matter how many times I imagined movies and awards, I thought about that look. It was the one imperfection in the whole day. And I couldn't figure it out. I was expecting jealousy, but that wasn't it. At least not the same kind of jealousy I'd seen from her before. If she was jealous, it was a really sad-jealous. I felt like I was trying to put together a puzzle without the box to show me the final picture.

Had she looked at me like that when I was performing?

I wasn't sure. I didn't think so. It was only when I was being congratulated by my mom and . . . dad.

Her dad.

So, sad-jealous?

Was that it?

Maybe her dad hadn't come to see Cassie be Juliet, and maybe he didn't film her or pretend she earned a trophy. Her parents were getting a divorce—or had gotten a divorce—and she said he hadn't been around. And maybe that hurt. A lot.

I'd heard that in some divorces the mom and the dad were still nice to each other and talked and supported their kids. But even so, it wouldn't be the same. And maybe some divorces weren't like that. Maybe Cassie's mom and dad didn't treat each other nice. I had heard of those too.

I sighed. That would be terrible. If my parents divorced, I would full-on, absolutely, nothing-held-back hate it.

Maybe Cassie hated it, too. Maybe that was why she'd given me that look. Maybe that was part of the reason she was so mean. She had always been a little selfish, but when her dad left, maybe that made things worse. A lot worse. It wasn't a good reason for Cassie to be mean, but I could see how it might have made it harder for her to be happy, to be nice.

I laid on my back and put my pillow over my face. I remembered how I felt when I found out about my tumor. How that had made it harder for me to be happy.

I remembered feeling afraid.

And I didn't want to be nice and smiley all the time. I definitely didn't want my friends to know about it; I thought they might not like me if they knew. Maybe that was kind of how Cassie felt. Lexi said that going through her parents' divorce was really hard on her. And no one gives you baskets full of gifts when your parents are going through a divorce. They don't put on mustaches for you. Cassie probably didn't feel like she had a huge cheerleading team. In fact, Cassie probably felt that she hardly had anyone in the world right now.

I didn't like that.

But she had been manipulative and mean. She had lied. Why would we be her friends? But I didn't like thinking about how she might feel.

And I didn't know what I should do about it.

# CHAPTER 38

## Seeing the Future

"Okay," I said. "I want to see further into the future." I had been staring into the oculator for the last few minutes, and depending on how my assistant changed the settings, parts of the future became clear to me. At first they were blurry, but with a few adjustments, I saw time machines, robot animals, and a chair that could read your mind. The future was going to be awesome.

"Is this one clearer, or this one?" my assistant asked.

I focused. "The second one."

Alright. I wasn't really looking into the future, but that's what it felt like with the huge, science fiction–looking goggles they put up to my eyes.

I was visiting the ophthalmologist. That's my favorite doctor name—and a fun word to say. *Ophthalmologist.* It means eye doctor.

Endocrinologist is a close second. That's the doctor that takes care of my hormones.

Say either word ten times fast. Try it.

I had to go to the ophthalmologist to get a prescription for my glasses. It had been six and a half weeks since my surgery, and my eyes had calmed down and healed enough that I was going to get glasses. Maybe I would get a pair with little mustaches on the side.

I had thought a lot about Cassie. I even asked Hannah to invite her to play with us. That took some convincing. I guess Cassie had said some mean things to Hannah, but I still thought Cassie was more likely to listen to Hannah than to me. It didn't work. And when Cassie said no, Hannah was so upset she told Cassie to never talk to her again.

I didn't know what to do next.

"Your eyes have changed a lot," the assistant said, bringing me back to the present. The ophthalmologist had asked her to start my testing and he would check in at the end. "Let me go and get the doctor. He can make sure that I'm seeing what I think I'm seeing." She got up quickly.

"What are you seeing?" Mom asked.

She hesitated. "Let me go and get the doctor."

I didn't like that hesitation or that answer. Soon my

ophthalmologist was in the room looking over my charts. He was a tall doctor guy with thick glasses. No mustache.

"Hey, Maddie," he said. And then he asked me a lot of the same questions doctors ask. How was I feeling? Did I eat a lot of ice cream when I was recovering? I noticed he looked over the information in my chart a lot of times, flipping back and forth through the pages. Then he asked different questions. I answered all of his "What letter do you see?" questions and looked up and down and left and right. He flipped through lenses on the cool machine, then lifted his own glasses and rubbed his eyes. "I'm going to send you across the street to the vision center and have them take pictures of the backs of your eyes. That will help me know for certain what I am seeing."

"What are you seeing?" Mom tried again.

"Let's look at those pictures first," he said. Was he stalling? Oh, no.

He wanted a scan. My insides knotted up instantly. I hated scans.

More questions.

And before I knew it, I was back in the escape pod machine getting another MRI.

When I came out, Dad was at the hospital with Mom. He'd rushed there straight from work.

Dr. Montoya was there too. "Your ophthalmologist noticed that your optical nerves are pinched again," she said, looking at a computer screen that showed the inside of my head. She still didn't show much emotion. "He wanted me to see into your head and figure out what is pinching them."

"The tumor is back?" I guessed, my stomach scrunching and twisting.

"Sort of." Dr. Montoya pulled up a picture of the front of my brain. "This little part here is all that is left of that tumor." She pointed to a tiny white sliver. "And we were hoping it would be a long time before it would do anything, but . . ."

But? But? I was desperate for her to finish her sentence.

She scrolled forward and backward between the MRI slides revealing different depths of my brain scan. She stopped on one. "Can you see this bubble here? This is what we call a cyst. It's not a tumor but more of a fluid-filled sac coming out of the tumor. And this cyst is pushing against your optical nerves here." She pointed each thing out very calmly. "Your brain is here. And what is left of your pituitary stem here."

*Pituitary* is another fun word to say. But it wasn't fun now. Nothing seemed fun now. I didn't fully understand everything she said, but I was almost holding my breath trying to figure out what all of it meant.

"And from how quickly the cyst appeared, it's very likely that it will continue to grow and cause you problems."

My heart started to pound. I knew what she was going to say.

"It's not wise to leave it there. We're going to have to do another surgery." The terrible words came out of her mouth like she was talking about me cleaning my room or doing my homework. I wondered if doctors practiced saying really hard things like they were just normal problems. But even though she said them all normal, the words echoed in my mind.

Another surgery.

*Surgery* is not a fun word. It isn't fun to say or to think about. I didn't want to say it ten times fast, and I definitely didn't want to do it again. It's a heavy word, a word that can smash stuff. Like a huge boulder tumbling down a hill and squashing a house, or a car, or all your happiness. I hated that word.

My monster was back. Scalier and uglier than ever. And bigger. A lot bigger. Right now, it felt like it could crush me with one stomp of its scaly foot.

I hadn't seen it coming when I looked into the future.

# CHAPTER 39

# Again

I was almost shaking under my mustache blanket.

Boo.

Super boo.

This time they were going to have to cut through my skull.
Yep. Through my skull. They had to use a drill for that. Gross.
And crazy. And painful. Thankfully medication would make
it so I didn't feel a thing. But this surgery would be scarier
than the first. The doctors couldn't go back through my nose
because there was a lot of scar tissue. I guess that meant my
body had blocked the way back as it healed. If they went that
way again, it would be extra-dangerous. So they were going

to shave a little part of my hair over my ear, cut a hole in my skull, and go under my brain to get to the cyst.

Ultra-nasty icky awful boo with rotten eggs and skunk-scented perfume on top. You can put all the mustaches you want on that and it isn't funny or happy or anything good.

My parents took me out for Shane's Shake Shack shakes again. My dad made me laugh, but most the time I forced it. And my mom talked about how this could be a blessing in disguise. Maybe the doctors could get the rest of the tumor while they were in there. Maybe after this, I wouldn't have to worry about the tumor anymore—ever.

But I knew that also meant that maybe some of those terrible things I worried might happen *last* time might really happen *this* time.

My brothers gave me big hugs when we got home. Max was the cutest. He hugged me supertight and said, "I wish my arms could be a huge mustache because then I could give you two things you really like at once." A mustache hug. Isn't that adorable? If adorable could kill a tumor and a cyst, this thing would be so dead. I love that kid. My brothers had all made me cards again, and this time no one asked for my candy or my money.

My mom lay on my bed with me until I fell asleep, but I woke up.

Again.

Staring up at my ceiling with the glow-in-the-dark stars

that weren't glowing very much anymore. It had been too long since I'd turned off the light.

In another two weeks.

Again.

Not a nightmare. Well, not a sleeping, dreaming one anyway. It was the real thing.

I knew I had friends. I knew I had a huge team on my side, but I didn't want to tell them again. I didn't want everyone to worry about me. I didn't even want another basket full of presents and notes. I just wanted it to go away.

I hadn't felt this bad in a long time. In fact, everything had been so good: my brothers actually treating me okay, my friends, my play, my parents. No one had it worse than me now. Not even Cassie.

She was in a bad situation, but not like this. She wasn't worried for her life. She wasn't worried about brain damage. But she was worried that everything might turn out terrible.

In fact, in a way, she might think it already had.

Maybe her family would never be the same again, never be together again. That would kind of be like having a surgery go wrong. Her brain wasn't damaged, but it probably felt like her family was.

And no one was rallying to her. Maybe she had wanted us to, but she had a terrible way of showing it. By lying to get what she wanted. By throwing parties so she could look good and get attention from boys. By excluding people because she was jealous. I remembered when she saw me passing out cards and I could tell she wanted one. That led her to make up another lie.

And she never apologized.

And that left her alone.

I rubbed my tired eyes. Then, lying in my bed in the dark, I had an idea. Turns out tumors and cysts can't stop ideas.

# CHAPTER 40

# Red, Sparkly Box

It took me almost the full two weeks to convince everyone, but eventually they did it. It was probably really hard to say no to the girl who had to go in for her second brain surgery.

And it gave me something else to think about. I really needed that.

I hoped it would do what it was supposed to do.

The bell for recess rang—my last recess before my second surgery—and my heart thumpy-thumped. I waited for everyone else to leave the room. Well, almost everyone.

"Are you sure you don't want us to go with you?" Yasmin asked.

I nodded.

"Okay," Lexi said. "Good luck. We'll be waiting for you."

"I'll catch up," I said. I would have put on a mustache to make me feel less nervous, but that would have messed everything up. I walked over to the counter, pulled out a big brown bag I'd brought from home, and started toward the door.

"Is everything okay?" Mrs. Baer asked, looking down at the bag in my hand. I guess going out to recess with a bag wasn't very common.

"I hope so," I said and left the room. I loved Mrs. Baer, but right then I didn't want to have to answer a bunch of questions.

As soon as I stepped out of the big doors into the sun, I had to blink lots of times. It was hard walking out into the brightness like that. I knew my friends were all gathering to hang out one more time, but I couldn't join them yet.

I walked the other direction. I almost started counting my steps toward the big spruce tree and the girl wearing a super-cute purple dress.

She saw me coming.

"Go away," Cassie called out while I was still a half a basketball court away.

I didn't answer. I just kept walking.

"Go away," she repeated.

"I will," I said. I was close enough that I didn't have to raise my voice. "But I need to do something first."

Cassie glared at me.

"A while ago," I continued, "I realized that maybe I'm not the only one who has to go through hard stuff." I blinked a little extra. "I think everyone does. It's just different versions of hard stuff. Like Devin's dad lost his job a few years ago. That had to be really hard." I nodded toward my group playing on the field. "And Lexi's parents got a divorce and that would be really difficult. Even Mrs. Baer had a sister who had to have a kidney transplant."

Cassie looked back at me with her best I-don't-care eyes.

I kept talking. "Sometimes we don't want others to know the bad stuff we're facing." I cleared my throat. "So I was thinking. I had a bunch of people cheering for me when I went through something hard. And I still do." They had all been asking me how I was and offered to give me another basket, but I'd kept all of their stuff from the first time. I didn't need anything else. "I wish everyone had that when life got ugly. I wish everyone had friends who told them it would be okay and tried to help out."

Cassie looked away. Was I boring her? Or did she just not want to listen?

Deep breath. I had no idea if this would work.

"I wanted to try to help," I said. "At least a little." I took a few steps closer to Cassie. That got her to look up at me again. "I'm going into surgery again tomorrow, but instead of having my friends give me more gifts or wear mustaches for me,

I asked them to do me a favor. Something for someone in my class who was going through a hard time."

I reached inside my big brown bag and pulled out a red, sparkly box I'd made. It said *Cards for Cassie* on the front in glittery, colorful letters I'd made myself. And it looked goooooood.

I set the box down in front of Cassie. She looked back at me, but this time her face was different. Not a glare, and not her sad-jealous look. Just different.

"They're cards. Lots of them. And they're all for you," I said. "And there's one in there from me. I owed you one." I pointed to the box, then turned and starting walking away.

I counted twenty steps before daring to look back, even though I was super curious and my heart was still thumping.

Cassie stared at the box, then glanced at me, and then back to the box.

I walked across the playground and joined up with my friends.

"Do you think she liked it?" Lexi asked.

"I don't know," I admitted. "She didn't seem to know what to think."

"I bet she liked it," Yasmin said.

I looked back over at Cassie, who was staring at the box. It took her another minute before she opened the first card.

No reaction. At least, not that I could tell. I was kind of far away.

She opened the second.

Nothing.

Then the third.

Nothing.

And then she started to bawl. Full-on, cry-her-eyes out bawling.

This was the second time I'd seen her crying underneath that tree. It was hard to tell, but I was pretty sure these tears were very different from the last. I think they were good tears. I think I can tell. I've cried all sorts of tears, so I'm kind of an expert.

I had convinced everyone to write Cassie a card and tell her anything nice about her they could think of. I told them she needed them. She was going through something hard too. She needed cards like I had needed mustaches.

And they'd done it.

Cassie brushed away her tears and read another card. I hoped her lips lifted up a little at the corners.

I hadn't read the cards, but I knew at least one of them invited Cassie to come hang out with us again, because it was the one I'd written.

# CHAPTER 41

## Epic

All my brothers were lined up and wearing mustaches. Well, not really lined up. More like standing in a glob.

"You'll do great," Christopher said and gave me a hug.

"Don't forget your hospital bag," Ethan said and brought it over to me. It had my clothes and books and movies for the hospital stay.

"We couldn't find the snack bag," Emery said. "It's gone missing." The snack bag was filled with granola bars and fruit and candy. If you're going to be stuck in a hospital room for several days, it's helpful to have a few snacks.

I saw it behind his legs.

"That's so weird," Ethan said. "I'm sure you'll do alright without it."

"It's behind you," Max ratted them out.

Emery put his finger to his lips.

"Oh!" Max said. "I mean, yeah, we couldn't find it."

Not much could make me smile before surgery again, but that did. This time we were going to the hospital the night before instead of waking up super early.

I gave them all tight hugs, including my Aunt Kimmie, who was babysitting the boys.

"Here you go," Max said and handed me a stick. "It's my magic wand. Just in case you need some, you know, magic. Usually it only works for me, but I put a spell on it so it can work for you for a while."

"Thanks," I said. I whirled it around and said a few made-up magic words, pretending to cast a spell. "Now, my magic slave," I said to Max, "go find me my bag of snacks."

He smiled big. "The magic doesn't work on me. It's my magic."

I looked at the wand. "Okay, well, maybe I'll try to use the magic on me."

"You got it," he said beaming.

I gave him another hug. Mom, Dad, and I said good-bye to my brothers one more time and picked up our bags.

As we walked out the door, my dad stopped so fast Mom and I almost bumped into him. There was a box on the porch, and Dad had almost stepped on it. "What's this?" he said. He picked up the box, then turned and handed it to me.

It was wrapped in blue-and-white paper, but it didn't have a bow or ribbon. There was a simple card. Three words were written in boy-handwriting.

## JUST IN CASE.

I opened the box. Inside was a bottle. A bottle I had seen before with the label "Antidote."

Devin.

I smiled again. I didn't think I'd be smiling so much today of all days. I wished he was here. I would probably hug him. But then he would feel embarrassed so maybe this way was better. Unless we hugged while wearing mustaches, then it would just be funny and not all awkward.

As I walked to the car, each step felt heavy. And that was after the hugs and smiles to cheer me up. Each step felt difficult even with the wand, the bag of snacks, and the antidote. This could be the worst thing I had to face. Worse than Dragoporkisaur. Worse than Orcalops. Worse than my last surgery. This was the climax. The time where I either turned out to be a glorious hero who triumphed over a dreaded challenge, or a tragic kid who fell in battle.

I had a monster to face.

All of a sudden, I stood in a field, the sun setting, and the

beat of my pounding heart matching the tremors of a ginormous beast stomping my way.

Seriously ginormous.

Bigger than it had ever been.

It was coming closer.

And closer.

Each step thundered through the ground.

I craned my neck, trying to see the top of this monster, and
with each earthshaking step, I was starting to get an idea of how
huge and horrifying it was. Its jaws gaped open wide enough to
swallow my city whole. Its eyes were like glowing fires, and its
whole body was covered in ugly, jagged scales. Down its back ran
spikes that looked like axe blades the size of two basketball courts.
Its clawed feet were bigger than shopping malls, and the claws
themselves were huge, each one the length of a tetherball pole.
They gouged the ground and rocks until they were dust.

The giant beast raised onto its hind legs and roared so
loudly the trees blew over and the tips of the mountains
crumbled. When it fell back down on all fours, the ground
rumbled and rolled like a giant wave. Boulders and houses flew
out of their places.

I told you it was ginormous. Seriously.

I had never faced anything like this.

But I had to. I had no choice.

Then it started to run. The terrifying monster stampeded
forward, its burning eyes focused on me.

I took a deep breath, then smiled.

Yep, I smiled.

This thing probably thought it had me beat. It probably had no idea that I wasn't just any girl.

No. Not even close.

I'm a ninja-centaur-princess with alien technology in my brain. And I sneeze lasers. I bet it won't see that coming. Plus, I had crossed the Sahara, finished secret missions, and escaped the Orcalops.

But I was pretty okay without that stuff, too. I had made new friends. I had stood up to Cassie, had a brain surgery, and performed Juliet while wearing a mustache. How many kids had done that?

Maybe I could do this.

It stomped closer.

And closer.

This wasn't like the last surgery. This one was bigger, harder.

I still had to try.

"You're going down, you crazy giant ugly monstrosity," I yelled. I didn't really know it *was* going down, but I figured I might as well sound confident.

"That's for sure," I heard a voice next to me.

"Definitely." Another voice on the other side.

I turned. My parents. Of course they were there. And they looked ready for a fight. My dad did a few of the karate moves he had used to scare away monsters when he was a kid. Maybe he wasn't a ninja like me, but it could help. My mom revved the engine of our minivan. She had pulled up right behind me and looked ready to drive right into the monster.

And then all my brothers ran up beside me. "Back down!" Christopher yelled. He sounded more intense than I'd ever heard him.

"Yeah." It was the twins. "You stupid, terrible, awful monster, you!" They took off their super-stinky socks and held them ready for battle. They could use all their almost-evilness against this terror.

"You leave my sister alone!" Max yelled. He pulled out another magic wand—apparently he had a backup—and then he turned himself into a puppy dragon. He was adorable even while he snarled and spewed out a thin stream of fire.

"No one is attacking Maddie while I can help it," Lexi said. She'd snuck up on me from the other side. She had glowing cards she was ready to throw at the monster. I hadn't seen glowing cards before, but I was sure they could do some damage.

"Especially not an ugly, nasty monster like you," Yasmin yelled at my nemesis. And then she burped out a bomb and caught it in her hand, ready to throw.

Revving.

A space cycle came from behind me. Devin. With a touch of a button, the guns and gadgets on the bike were ready for attack. Cesar swooped in with his jet pack. Then Sailor and Hannah, each in their space gear. One by one all sorts of kids in my class showed up with something they could hurl at the monster.

"Back off," a loud voice sounded, followed by roars. I looked back to see Mrs. Baer riding on a bear. She had a whole posse of them behind her. They snarled and roared, ready to run in for the attack.

Maybe there was a chance. Maybe I could face this thing. Maybe we could face it together.

With the monster thumping closer, I called out a battle cry, and we all charged, screaming, our weapons ready. With each step, my heart pounded harder.

And if all else failed, I still had the antidote.

Just before I came face-to-face with the beast—okay, more like face-to-foot—I caught a glimpse of a light to my side, something shiny. I glanced over, not able to tell for sure, but I thought I could see something coming from beyond the horizon. It glinted like a crown. Maybe it was the queen of my school, on her way to join us.

I really hoped so.

I didn't know how the fight would turn out, but I knew I had some of the best family and friends in the world. And we wouldn't give up.

This battle was going to be epic!

# Acknowledgments

Thank you to Shadow Mountain. They were releasing Chad's first book when Maddie went into surgery, and they were amazingly supportive, helping juggle his tour cancellations and rescheduling him where they could. They were patient and helpful. They wore mustaches for Maddie and wrote encouraging emails and always wanted to know how she was doing. They even assembled quite the gift basket for her.

We especially need to thank Chris Schoebinger, Lisa Mangum, and Heidi Taylor. They invited us to write this book, believed in it, and gave us priceless feedback on several drafts to help the story come together. Thanks for believing in this story.

We also owe thanks to Heather Ward for her amazing cover and Richard Erickson for the art direction. Lisa Mangum did more work for us as our editor. Ben Grange gave great advice and counsel and help as our agent. Peggy Eddleman, Jennie Bennett, Kimberley Johnson, Sharon Brown, and Madelyn Morris were fantastic beta readers.

And thanks to Maddie for letting us write this story. She read and approved it. And thanks to our sons who were a great support to Maddie and who let us write about their stinky feet and licking toothbrushes.

And again, thank you to everyone who helped our daughter, who made the real-life story the miracle it was.

# Authors' Note

This book was based on the true story of our daughter, Maddie. She thinks fake mustaches are hilarious, has a great sense of humor, and loves to act in plays. In February 2013, she was diagnosed with a tumor on her pituitary gland pressing up against her brain. She courageously faced a very difficult situation, went through one successful surgery, and then later had to face another. Her brothers (she really has four brothers, and two of them are identical twins), teachers (Mrs. Acord and Mrs. Lyon), and friends were extremely supportive.

People really did put on mustaches, took pictures, and sent them to her or posted them on the Internet with the hashtag #mustachesformaddie. (It was Jenny Mason's idea. Thanks, Jenny, and thanks to everyone who made our girl smile.) There were hundreds, if not thousands. A few local news stations even did stories about it. All those mustaches definitely cheered Maddie up.

We will forever love her doctors, William T. Couldwell and Jay Riva-Cambrin, and the staffs of Primary Children's Hospital and the University of Utah Hospital. They pulled off a miracle for our girl.

Maddie also faced pressures and problems in school, though Cassie and the difficult situations that happened at the elementary school in this book were entirely made up. Though Yasmin, Lexi, Devin, and others were fictional characters, Maddie had many real friends who helped her. And Maddie did make up games to get more kids involved in her school.

Chad, the father in the story, really was in a hospital room with his girl when his debut novel hit the shelves. He had to cancel part of his promotional tour and doesn't regret it at all.

Near the end of 2014, Maddie had a second surgery, and her doctors were able to not only remove a cyst that had grown on the remaining tumor tissue, but miraculously, they also removed the rest of her tumor. As of 2017, no signs of the tumor have returned, though Maddie still has an MRI regularly to check. She was an amazing girl before the surgery and has grown to become even stronger, braver, and more caring through her experience.

To all those out there who face something extremely challenging, may you also face it with good family and friends, a strong imagination, lots of prayers, and maybe even a few mustaches. Good luck!

# Letter from Maddie

Hello fellow readers,

I hope you liked this book. It is kind of weird having a book based on me, but it's also pretty cool.

You've read about the story version of me. I wanted you to know the real me. I do really like potatoes and mustaches and acting in plays. And my elementary school really did do scenes from Shakespeare. I wasn't Juliet, though; I was Petruchio from *Taming of the Shrew*. I got to wear a long golden cape and a cool hat. And my friend even drew a mustache on my face. It was pretty awesome. I also like to read, draw, and crochet.

Even though Cassie isn't based on a real person and some of the situations at school in this book are different from my life, I did have troubles with some girls, and I really did make up games to help me make new friends, including Claire, Ashley, Emma, Nieve, Lauren, Aubrey, and Kate. The part about my tumor is pretty accurate except the surgeries were about a year and half apart, instead of months.

I think everyone who reads this book should realize the moral of the story is . . .

Drum roll please . . .

To love potatoes and mustaches!

Okay, probably not really. There's more to it.

I learned a lot through my friend troubles and surgeries. Like, small acts of kindness can go a long way. A really long way. And when things are rough, you can always find a way to laugh.

I try really hard to be friends with everyone. We don't always realize what trials other people are going through. Sometimes it takes courage to be kind to some people. But we need to always stick up for what's right. You can do it. Anytime, anywhere, you can have compassion. Everybody needs a friend and that friend can be you. So show them that you truly care.

Be kind. Smile more. Laugh more. Dream more.

Thanks for reading,

Maddie

# Discussion Questions

1. Maddie loves mustaches because they make her laugh. What do you love? What makes you laugh?

2. What did you think of Cassie? Have you ever been in a situation where someone didn't welcome others to hang out with them? How did it make you feel? What did you do?

3. Maddie wanted to stand up for Lexi, but she didn't have the courage. Why is it sometimes hard to stand up for others? Why do you think it might be worthwhile to make sure that others are invited to hang out instead of walking around alone?

4. Maddie has a large family. What is your family like? How many siblings do you have? How well do you get along with

them? How do they help you through hard times? How do you help them?

5. In Maddie's class, a lot of the students are excited about doing scenes from Shakespeare's plays. Have you ever been in a play? Did you like it? Why or why not? Have you ever read or seen any of Shakespeare's plays? What did you think of them?

6. Lexi was a new girl in school and didn't have many friends. Have you ever been the new kid in school? What was good about it? What was difficult? Do you have anyone in your class or grade who is new this year? How might you be able to help them?

7. When Maddie struggled with her arm and leg, she had to go to the doctor. She felt nervous in several of the medical situations. When have you been to the doctor? How did you feel?

8. Maddie discovered that she had a tumor pressing against her brain. What did Maddie learn from going through that challenge? What is a challenge you have had to face? What did you learn from going through that difficult experience?

9. Maddie didn't want her teacher or her class to know about her tumor. If you were in Maddie's situation, would you want others to know? Have you ever had a difficult problem that you didn't want to share with others? When do you think it's a good idea to share and when isn't it?

10. Maddie's friends and family put on mustaches to encourage her. Lexi, Maddie, and others also wrote cards to cheer up Cassie. Do you know someone who could use some cheering up or encouragement? What could you do for them?

11. Maddie has a great imagination and uses it to deal with her challenges. Do you have a great imagination? How does your imagination help you?

12. Maddie made up a few new playground games, including Poison Dragon Death Claw and Supernova. Have you ever made up a new game? What was it like? If you had to make up a new game, what would it be?

# About the Authors

Chad Morris and Shelly Brown are the proud parents of four sons and one daughter, Maddie, who was diagnosed with a brain tumor when she was nine.

Chad grew up wanting to become a professional basketball player or a rock star. Neither of those plans quite panned out, so he wrote and performed sketch comedy while going to college. Now he's a teacher and a writer.

Shelly loves to write books for children. In her spare time, she enjoys the theater and traveling. In addition to her five children, she has three chickens and sixty-four Pez dispensers.

# Praise for
## *Mustaches for Maddie*

Nominated for Rhode Island Children's Book Award and
Ohio Buckeye Children's Book Award

"A moving story of courage and heart."
—*PUBLISHERS WEEKLY*

"This sweet, hopeful, believable, and unsentimental tale rings
true. Being brave, growing up, true friendship—this has it all."
—*BOOKLIST*

"Very funny yet poignant, an encouraging read."
—*BOOKPAGE*

"A humorous and heartfelt story of a courageous girl determined
to face her troubles with a smile."
—JENNIFER A. NIELSEN, *New York Times* bestselling author

"Warm and witty . . . a beautifully quirky story, honestly told,
that is full of heart and love and power."
—CARRIE JONES, *New York Times* bestselling author of the
Need series

"Based on the true story of the authors' daughter, who was diagnosed with a brain tumor. *Mustaches for Maddie* is good for any
kid facing challenges: whether at home or at school."
—JESSICA DAY GEORGE, *New York Times* bestselling author
of *Wednesdays in the Tower*

"An endearing tale. Maddie will make you laugh, fill your heart,
and somehow leave you better than before you knew her story."
—RICHARD PAUL EVANS, #1 *New York Times* bestselling
author of the Michael Vey series

"*Mustaches for Maddie* is an incredible story full of love, humor, and courage. Her determination to face challenges will leave you feeling stronger."

—TYLER WHITESIDES, author of Janitors series

"*Mustaches for Maddie* is full of heart, hope, and humor. I laughed and cried, cheered and worried, and wished I'd had a friend like Maddie when I was in sixth grade. This is a must-read book for anyone facing challenges of their own."

—PEGGY EDDLEMAN, author of Sky Jumpers series

"*Mustaches for Maddie* is a thoroughly enjoyable testament to the power of laughter and compassion."

—J. SCOTT SAVAGE, author of Mysteries of Cove series

"You'll cheer for Maddie in this emotional (and truly funny) story about a real hero taking on life's hardest challenges."

—FRANK COLE, author of *The Afterlife Academy*

"The quirky humor combined with emotional depth made *Mustaches for Maddie* one of the most refreshing, original, and enjoyable books I've read in a long while."

—LIESL SHURTLIFF, *New York Times* bestselling author of
    *Red: The True Story of Red Riding Hood*